CAPTAIN ★AWESOME
TO THE RESCUE

CAPTAIN ★AWESOME
VS. NACHO CHEESE MAN

CAPTAIN ★AWESOME
AND THE NEW KID

CAPTAIN ★AWESOME
VS. THE SPOOKY SCARY HOUSE

By STAN KIRBY

Illustrated by
GEORGE O'CONNOR

LITTLE SIMON
New York   London   Toronto   Sydney   New Delhi

This book is a work of fiction. Any references to historical events, real people, or real places are used fictitiously. Other names, characters, places, and events are products of the author's imagination, and any resemblance to actual events or places or persons, living or dead, is entirely coincidental.

 LITTLE SIMON
An imprint of Simon & Schuster Children's Publishing Division
1230 Avenue of the Americas, New York, New York 10020
This Little Simon hardcover edition May 2016
Captain Awesome to the Rescue, Captain Awesome vs. Nacho Cheese Man, and
Captain Awesome and the New Kid copyright © 2012 by Simon & Schuster, Inc.
Captain Awesome vs. the Spooky, Scary House copyright © 2013 by Simon & Schuster, Inc. All rights reserved, including the right of reproduction in whole or in part in any form. LITTLE SIMON is a registered trademark of Simon & Schuster, Inc., and associated colophon is a trademark of Simon & Schuster, Inc.
For information about special discounts for bulk purchases, please contact Simon & Schuster Special Sales at 1-866-506-1949 or business@simonandschuster.com.
The Simon & Schuster Speakers Bureau can bring authors to your live event. For more information or to book an event contact the Simon & Schuster Speakers Bureau at 1-866-248-3049 or visit our website at www.simonspeakers.com.
Designed by Laura Roode
The text of this book was set in Little Simon Gazette.
Manufactured in the United States of America 0416 FFG
2 4 6 8 10 9 7 6 5 3 1
Library of Congress Control Number 2015959775
ISBN 978-1-4814-7603-4
ISBN 978-1-4424-3562-9 (*Captain Awesome to the Rescue* eBook)
ISBN 978-1-4424-3564-3 (*Captain Awesome vs. Nacho Cheese Man* eBook)
ISBN 978-1-4424-4201-6 (*Captain Awesome and the New Kid* eBook)
ISBN 978-1-4424-7256-3 (*Captain Awesome vs. the Spooky, Scary House* eBook)

These titles were previously published individually in hardcover and paperback by Little Simon.

Contents

Table of Contents

"**W**here's my Captain Awesome cape?" Eugene grumbled as he searched his closet. He tossed clothes back over his head, covering a stack of Super Dude comic books.

Psssst! Want to know a secret? It's the most hugest, gigantist, enormondoist secret ever. The boy looking for his cape is not just eight-year-old Eugene McGillicudy, son of Ned and Betsy, and brother to his little sister, Molly. He's also the superhero known as Captain Awesome!

Say it out loud:

CAPTAIN! AWESOME!

Eugene came up with that name himself. That's one of the cool things about being a superhero. You get to pick your own name. And if you're making up your own superhero name, it shouldn't be something lame like "Captain Just Okay." It should be mighty, like . . . Captain Awesome! MI-TEE!

Eugene plopped on the pile of clothes and crossed his arms. *Next time, I'll remember to follow Superhero Rule number one: Never let your mom pack your superhero*

stuff when you're moving to a new town. I bet Super Dude's mom never lost his cape.

Wait! You've never heard of Super Dude?! He's only THE coolest, bravest, heroist superhero of all time, and the one responsible for Eugene becoming Captain Awesome.

It all started the day Eugene's dad gave him his copy of Super Dude No. 1.

Sure, it might've looked like he was just giving Eugene the comic so he wouldn't tell his mother who ate the last of the chocolate-chocolate chip ice cream, but Eugene knew what his dad was secretly telling him: Since he's too busy with work and

dad-stuff like mowing lawns and telling Eugene to keep his elbows off the dinner table, and eating the last of his mom's chocolate-chocolate chip ice cream, it was up to Eugene to save the world from now on!

Eugene and his family had just moved to a new town called Sunnyview for his dad's job—he worked for Cherry Computers. ("Cherry's on Top!")

"Eugene!" his mom called from downstairs. "Can you please come down when you get a chance? I want to talk to you about school."

Oh, great! First she loses my cape and now she wants to talk about school! Eugene looked at the calendar on his wall. *And tomorrow's my first day.*

Hooray.

BY HOORAY I REALLY MEAN BARF! I DON'T

SUPER DUDE RETURNS!

SCHOOL !

WANT TO GO TO A NEW SCHOOL!

Eugene fell backward into his clothes pile and covered his head with his pajamas.

Things were really getting desperate! First his cape was missing, and now school talk?! Yuck! Could today get any worse?!

Eugene leaped to his feet and struck a superhero pose. "Miff ivnent da mime poo burry abut barf—" Eugene stopped and yanked the pajamas off his face. "This isn't the time to worry about BARF and new schools,"

Eugene said and punched his hand into his palm. "I need to find my cape or Captain Awesome won't be able to protect Sunnyview from the evil doings of bad guys like Queen Stinkypants, Baron Von Booger, or Dr. Spinach. Letting the bad guys win is

worse than
homework ...
on a weekend!"

Evildoers all over
Sunnyview had better
beware, because Captain
Awesome was going to ferret them
out just like a, well, a ferret ferrets
stuff, except he'll be wearing a
superhero outfit and he won't
have a furry tail.

Captain Awesome will give bad

guys his famous one-two punch
and tell them to change their ways
and become good guys . . . or . . .
he'll . . . tell their parents.

And if you think the Captain Awesome one-two punch sounds scary, you should see a super-villain's angry parents. Bad guys hate to lose, but they hate being grounded even more!

But instead of fighting evil this morning, Eugene was digging through all the boxes in his new bedroom looking for his superhero cape.

"I'll bet Super Dude never had days like this." Eugene sighed.

And that's when Eugene heard it! The evil "Goo!" and "Gaaah!"

of his archenemy . . . **Queen Stinkypants from Planet Baby!**

CHAPTER 2

The Attack of Queen Stinkypants!

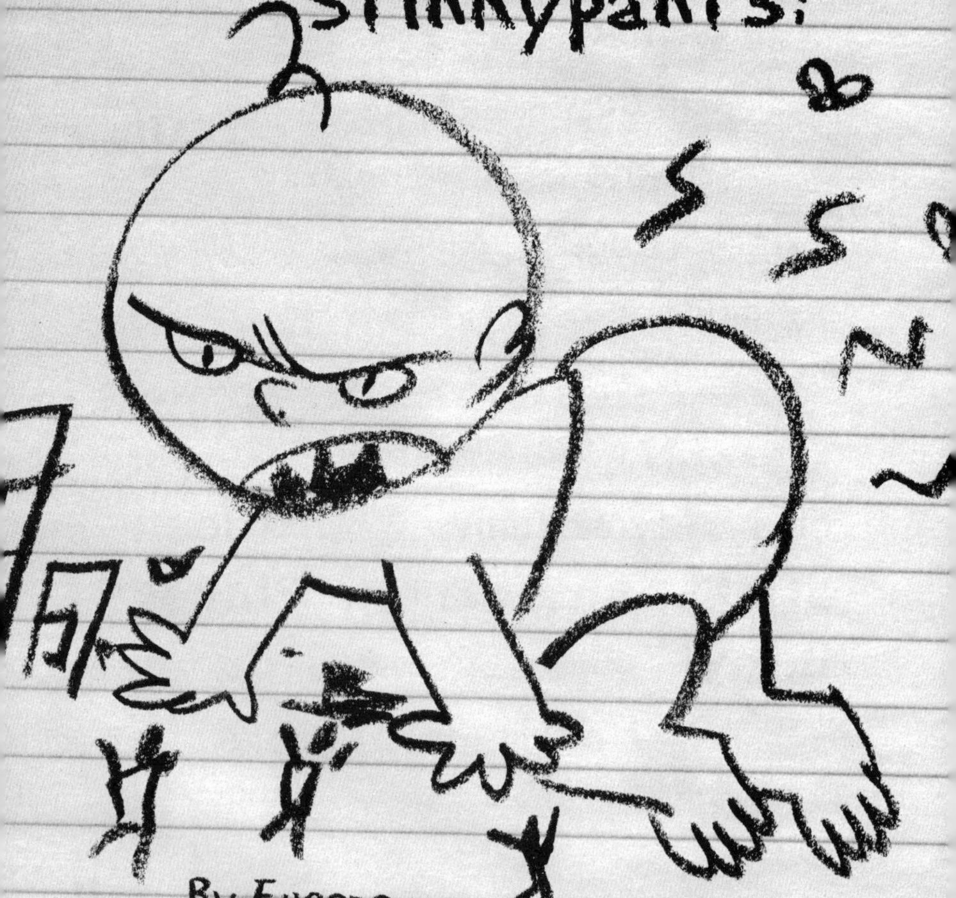

Left foot. Right foot. "Goo." Fall down. Get up. Left foot. Right foot. Fall down. "Gaah." Get up.

"I'd know those sounds anywhere!" Eugene raced to his bedroom door and peeked down the hallway . . . and there she was! "QUEEN STINKYPANTS!" he cried. "My archenemy from Planet Baby!"

 Even from the safety of his secret hideout,

Eugene could smell the terrible stink of her stinky stink powers! Blech!

"She followed me to Sunnyview! She found my secret hideout! She'll discover my secret identity!" wailed Eugene. Then he realized the worst thing of all! "AHHHH! She'll drool all over my toys! For the sake of all the arms and legs of my action figures, and the safety of the universe,

I have to stop her!"

Eugene jumped onto his bed. He stuck out his chest and thrust his fist into the sky, just like he had seen Super Dude do on the cover of Super Dude No. 7 when he fought the Society of Evil Babysitters.

"Queen Stinkypants must never, ever, ever, nope, never enter my secret base! So vows Captain Awesome! Heroes don't let villains

do that . . . especially stinky super-villains because you'll never get the smell out of your carpet!"

She would not, COULD NOT be allowed to enter the room. Captain Awesome doesn't like bad guys, and he also doesn't like cleaning his room.

Eugene raced to his closet and grabbed his Captain Awesome suit. Quickly, he tried to pull it on over his tennis shoes. That didn't work! He lost his balance.

"ACK!" he yelled as he fell to the floor.

"Hey! There you are!" Eugene's
cape was under the bed! Standing up, he flipped the cape over his
head . . . and couldn't see a thing.
The cape covered his face!

He bumped into his bed and fell
to the floor, again.

BONK!

That was either the sound of his head hitting the floor or THE SOUND OF QUEEN STINKY-PANTS at his door! Eugene fixed his cape as the door flung open. A blast of evil, stinky, smelly baby came at him.

"Ugh." Eugene made that face you make when you see brussels sprouts. YUCKY!

"Bwaaa-goo-baaa-gene-daaada!"

Queen Stinkypants babbled in her secret, evil baby language.

Eugene knew what every sound meant though. After she stunk up his room, she was going to drool on everything he held most dear. He had to protect his army of action figures and his collection of Super Dude comic books.

GROSS!

"No drooling on my watch, villain!" Eugene called out. Captain Awesome, and his cape, leaped into action!

CHAPTER 3

Evil Wears Pink Ribbons in Its Hair!

By Eugene

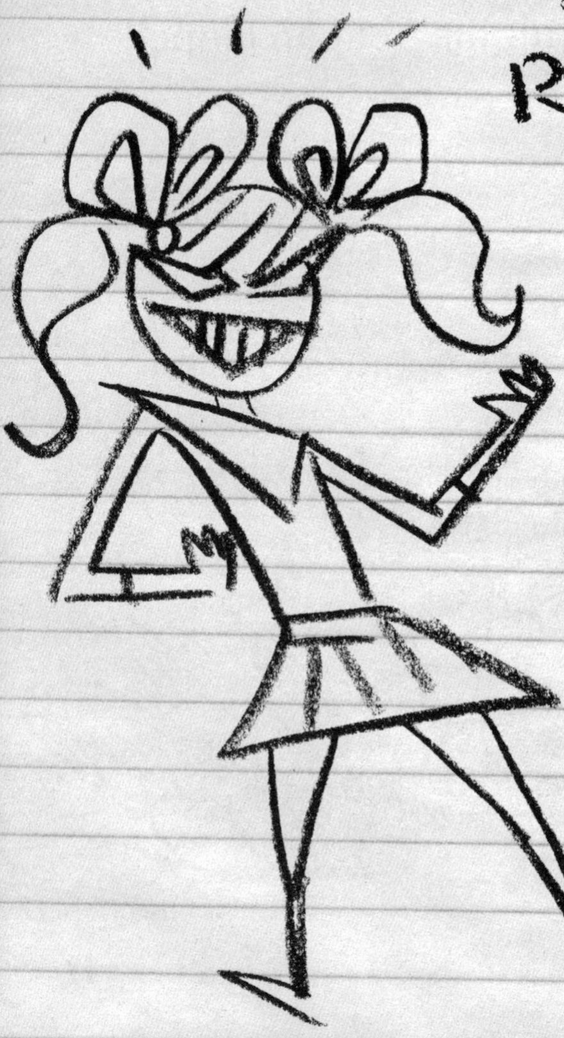

Riiiiing!

"Arrgh!" Eugene cried out.

The school bell! Was it the first bell or the second bell at Sunnyview Elementary School? Was he on time or later than late? Being late was bad, but being later than late, and on the first day at a new school, was the worst. Like green-bean-ice-cream-covered-in-broccoli-mush-sauce worse.

And just as YUCKY! Eugene cracked open the door to the school hallway. Hallways were a danger zone where the principal or vice principal patrolled— a duo of doom that would like to lock up a late student in their DUNGEON OF DETENTION. Together they would wait like furry little spiders hungry for a buzzing late fly with a backpack.

STOMP! STOMP-STOMP!

Footsteps echoed
down the empty hall!
Only a principal would
wear shoes that
STOMPED so . . .

loud . . . or someone wearing bricks on their feet. *Oh no! What if the principal's shoes are made of bricks?* Eugene gasped. *What kind of school is this place?*

Eugene dove into the nearest classroom to avoid Principal Brick Foot. He ducked as the principal lumbered by. *STOMP! STOMP-STOMP!* echoed down the hall.

"You'll never catch me, Principal Brick Foot." Eugene chuckled.

"Can I help you?" a voice behind him asked.

Eugene spun from the door and

faced . . . a **TEACHER.**

"N-no," he stammered. "I was just hiding from Principal Brick Foot." The class laughed. Eugene's fingers dug into his backpack, clutching it tighter to his chest.

"I'll bet you're Eugene McGillicudy," Ms. Beasley, the teacher, said.

Eugene gasped. *How could she know that?* And then he realized the worstest, awfulest truth: *She can read minds!* Eugene grabbed his head to

stop her from sucking more thoughts from his brain.

Ms. Beasley held up her right hand and the class stopped giggling. "Eugene, I have your name on my roll sheet as the new student. Why don't you tell us *all* about yourself?"

Eugene looked around, hoping there was another new boy named Eugene standing behind him. *I'll bet Super Dude never has*

to stand in front of class and talk about *himself*, Eugene thought. *I also bet Super Dude doesn't have a brain-sucker for a teacher.*

"Ha-ha-ha!" Meredith Mooney laughed. "The new kid is a scaredy-

pants. Oh, please tell us about your oh-so-special self, Eugene. Won't you, please? My ears can't wait!"

"Meredith. Please be polite," Ms. Beasley said.

Eugene guessed that Meredith's mother must've tied the pink ribbons in her hair too tight. That would explain a lot about how she was acting.

"We are all waiting, Eugene," Ms. Beasley reminded.

Then Eugene realized something more awful than a babysitter with bad breath! The teacher and

Meredith were working together.

Like Super Dude always said:

"OHHH NO!"

Ms. Beasley had to be **MISS BEASTLY**, yet another villain destined to do really bad stuff to the mighty Captain Awesome . . . and the universe. *Like give me really hard homework, Eugene realized. Every night . . . just for fun!*

Not today, villain! Eugene was on to her secret plan. Ms. Beastly *wanted* him to tell everyone about himself so he'd reveal his secret identity as Captain Awesome! She

was using her evil sidekick, **Little Miss Stinky Pinky,** to tease him into doing it!

Looks like it was time to send evil to bed without its dessert. Miss Beastly and Little Miss Stinky Pinky would be no match for the awesomest power of **Captain Awesome!**

MI-Tee!

CHAPTER 4

Introducing Turbo

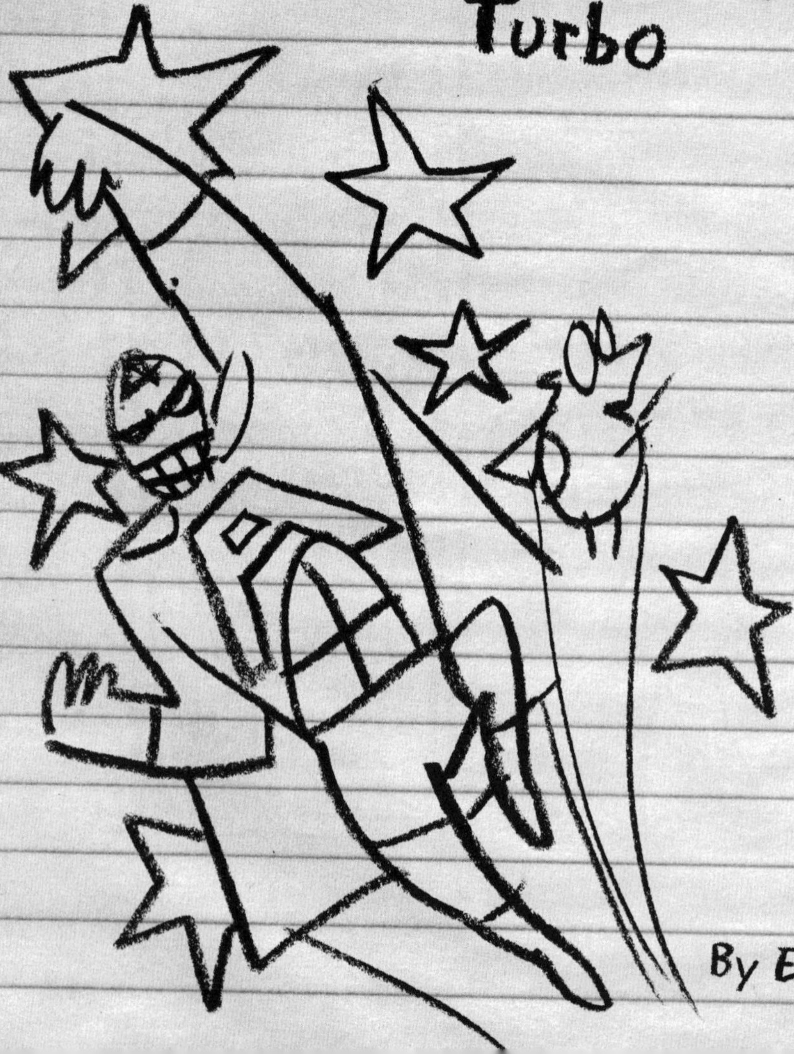

By Eugene

Eugene's second day at school was much like his first: a ringing bell and a narrow escape from Principal Brick Foot. Meredith Mooney called him Pizza Breath. So what if Eugene liked to sneak leftover pizza from the fridge for breakfast? Ms. Beasley once again called on him to stand in front of the class.

That's when

things got weirder than a frog with three eyes and a purple cowboy hat.

"How would you like to be in charge of Turbo?" Ms. Beasley asked.

What was this Operation Turbo? Some kind of supervillain trap? Was Eugene being called on to save the school? To turn up the air-conditioning? To find out what was being served for lunch today? That was easy. Something GROSS!

"Turbo?" Eugene said. "What's a turbo?"

"Turbo is our class pet. He's a hamster." Ms. Beasley pointed to a cage in the back of the room. A little brown-and-white hamster was happily spinning on his squeaky metal exercise wheel.

Eugene paused. *Definitely* a trap.

"He? What?! Turbo?! I'm supposed to take care of Turbo!" Meredith whined, clearly unhappy with Ms. Beasley's choice.

"My! Me! Mine! Mere-DITH!"

"I'll do it!" Eugene blurted. Even if it was a trap, if it made Meredith unhappy, Eugene was ready to go! Eugene's heart soared like Super Dude's after that time he put Commander Barf Face in space jail in issue No. 34.

Meredith, like many villains, had a calendar to prove it was her turn to care for the little furry creature.

Unfortunately, she held it too close to Turbo's cage. The roly-poly hamster grabbed her calendar in his paws and started chomping so fast that Eugene understood why he was called "Turbo."

Turbo stopped chewing and looked up at Eugene. *Did the hamster just smile?*

"I really like this hamster," Eugene said. He was also starting to think that maybe, just maybe, Ms. Beasley wasn't so bad after all.

There was one thing about Sunnyview that was the same as Eugene's old school. He could smell the Mystery Meatloaf Surprise long before he saw it.

Eugene got his lunch and went to find a seat.

There was a sinking feeling in his stomach, and it wasn't from the smell of the Mystery Meatloaf Surprise.

It was that

horrible feeling that all new kids
get . . . where to sit in the cafeteria.
Meredith and her friends sat at one
table. No chance Eugene would sit
with them. There was an open seat
next to Mike Flinch, but he smelled
like Eugene's grandpa who spent

most of his time in his backyard digging for lost pirate treasure.

"Hey, Eugene! Yo! Over here!" Charlie Thomas Jones called out. Charlie was the one boy who *didn't* laugh when Meredith Mooney was teasing Eugene.

Eugene put down his tray and sat. Charlie brought his own lunch. He had two cans of squirt cheese and a stack of crackers. He squirted little cheese mountains on top of each cracker.

"You sure do like cheese,"

Eugene commented.

"It's better than that stuff." Charlie pointed at the rectangle on Eugene's tray. "You're eating the Mystery Meatloaf Surprise."

If a supervillain ever created a blob of gooey garbage to rob Eugene of his Captain Awesome powers, it would probably look a lot like the grayish-brown meat-thing sitting on Eugene's tray. "What's the surprise?" Eugene asked.

"You'll find out," Charlie said. "You must have an iron stomach stronger than Super Dude to eat that stuff."

"Super Dude?" Eugene was shocked. "You know who Super Dude is?"

"I have every one of his comic books!" Charlie proudly said. "I've also got a Super Dude action figure on my dresser and this talking Super Dude watch." Charlie pressed a button on his watch.

"Danger is my middle name!" the watch announced.

"Super Dude's my most favorite superhero EVER!" Eugene liked Charlie, but he wasn't sure if it was a good idea to tell him about his secret identity as Captain Awesome just yet.

Eugene took a bite of his meatloaf and made a *yuck* face.

"Surprise!" Charlie laughed.

Eugene laughed, then gagged. He spit out his bite of Mystery Meatloaf Surprise and hid it under a pile of corn. At least, he *thought* it was corn. . . .

CHAPTER 6

The Lost Hamster Weekend

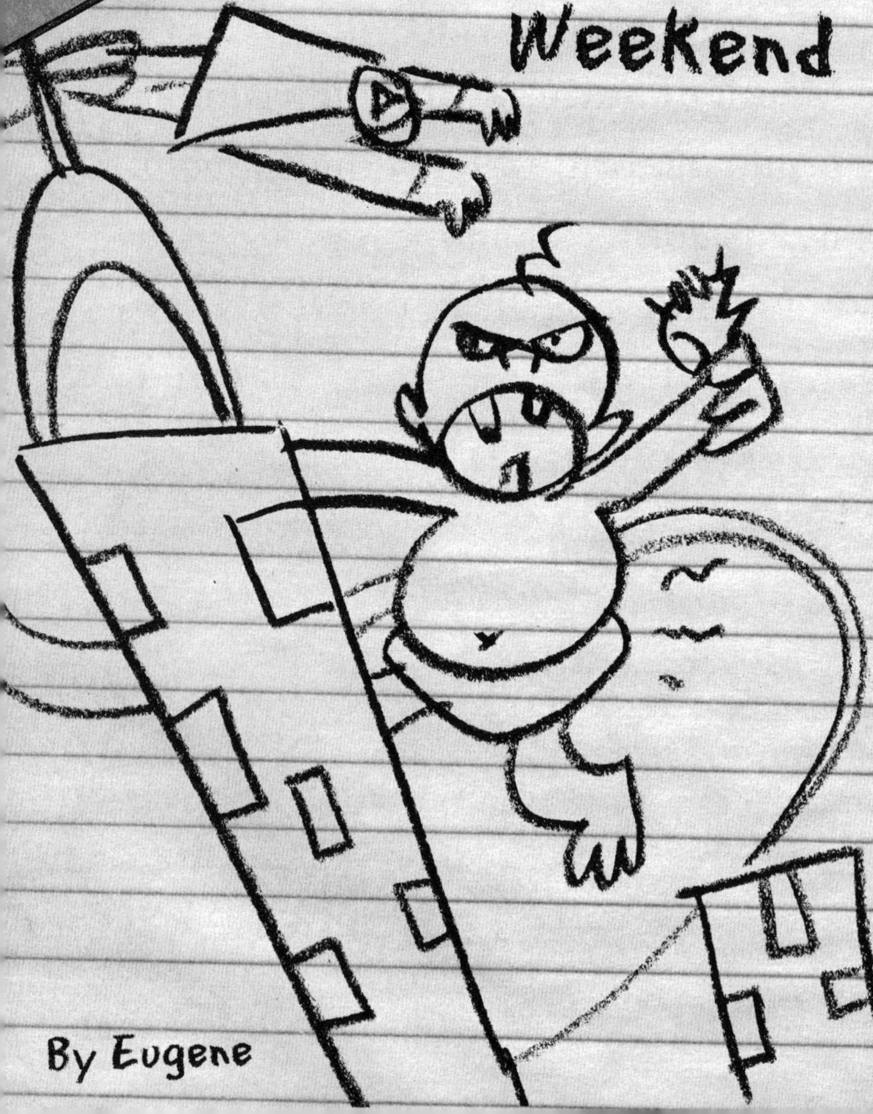

Ms. Beasley had given Eugene a job, and he was going to do it right. That weekend he took Turbo home and introduced him to Mom, Dad, and Molly.

Eugene kept the cage in his bedroom, and whenever he left, he loaded Turbo into his round, plastic hamster ball—the Turbomobile—so

that Turbo could follow him. Turbo joined him at the swing set, by the bathtub, and even at the dinner table.

"At least *he* keeps his cute little elbows off the table," Eugene's mom said, pointing to Turbo.

Eugene even shared his secret with his new friend.

"Turbo," Eugene whispered. "I know I can trust you with a secret, mostly because no one understands Hamster, but I want you to feel safe here because underneath these matching clothes, I'm really . . . **CAPTAIN AWESOME!**"

Turbo unleashed a tiny squeak, and Eugene smiled. A hamster's squeak was as good as a handshake, and he knew his secret would be safe.

But Sunday morning brought trouble.

Eugene slept late, sleeping sounder than Super Dude's sidekick Sergeant Super Bear during his winter hibernation in deep space.

When Eugene finally woke up, he reached over to Turbo's cage on the nightstand.

"Good morning, Turbo!" Eugene said happily. "Let's see what Mom made for breakfast! Will it be Pancakes of Power or Titanium French Toast?"

But Turbo didn't squeak an answer! He was gone!

"Turbo!" Eugene yelled. "Where are you?" Eugene jumped to his feet and pounded his fist into his palm. "This has to be the wicked work of the most super of duper supervillains . . . ever! Which one could it be?"

Eugene thought for a moment. *Superheroes have a lot of enemies, but who hamsternapped his friend Turbo?*

And more importantly, how could Eugene face Ms. Beasley and the rest of his class if they knew that Turbo was missing?

"Blah blah blah! Toldja so-

toldja so-toldja so! Yackity yack yack!" He could already hear Meredith's teasing.

For the sake of Turbo—and the fear of Meredith's "nyah nyah nyah nyah nyahs"—he had to find Turbo before it was too late.

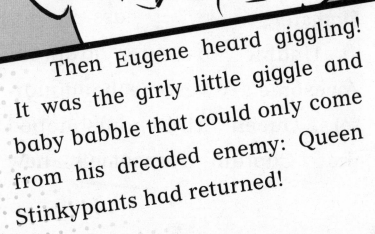

Then Eugene heard giggling! It was the girly little giggle and baby babble that could only come from his dreaded enemy: Queen Stinkypants had returned!

The giggling came from behind the door at the end of the hall. Eugene wondered what Queen Stinkypants was up to. And then it hit him!

Queen Stinkypants can speak Hamster!

Unable to enter Captain Awesome's awesome headquarters, Queen Stinkypants hoped that Captain Awesome's new friend, Turbo, would reveal all of Captain Awesome's awesome secrets.

Eugene raced back to his room to get his Captain Awesome outfit. Super Dude would never leave his outfit in a pile on the floor of *his* bedroom! That's because

superheroes are supposed to keep their bedrooms clean—especially if they still live with their parents.

Eugene ran quickly into his closet and changed into his Captain Awesome outfit.

"MI-TEE!" He shouted and ran smack into the door, bounced off, crashed into the bed, and fell to the floor.

Oops! I forgot about the door!

Captain Awesome opened the door, ran down the hallway, and grabbed the doorknob to Queen Stinkypants's Cosmic Stink Ship.

He could smell the familiar stinky stink of stinky stuff.

"Isn't it ever bathtime for supervillains?" Captain Awesome wondered. He pinched his nose and threw open the door.

"Get your diapery hands off that hamster!" Captain Awesome warned.

"Gaaah! Bwaaaah maaa moo beeemooo!" Queen Stinkypants answered.

And then Captain Awesome saw the most horrible thing possible except for the time Jill

Finbender tried to kiss him in first grade.

Turbo sat at a tiny table with Queen Stinkypants. He wore a mind-control baby bonnet and was about to be served a cup of tea!

"AAAAAAAAH! Don't drink that tea, Turbo!" Captain Awesome shouted. "It's got extra sugar in it so you can't taste the evil!"

CHAPTER 7

1 Boy - 1 Hamster = Bad News

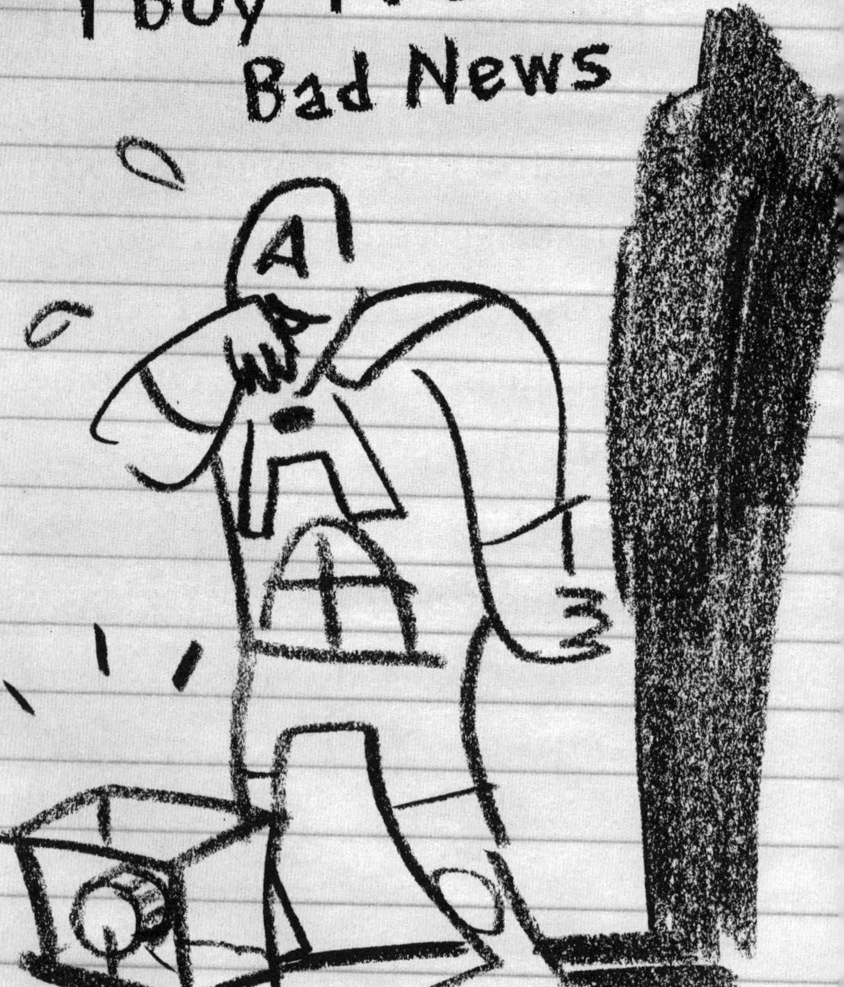

by Eugene

2+2= AWESOME!

Eugene was tired of thinking about how many apples he'd have if he started with four then added twelve and divided everything by four. Who wants that many apples?

Superheroes don't need math, Eugene thought. *That's why they punch things! Superheroes need to be outside so they can swing and climb on stuff.*

The bell rang. Everyone ran for the door like they were chasing after free chocolate. Eugene waited for the classroom to empty, then headed over to Turbo's cage.

"Today's a very special day," Eugene whispered. "I want you to be Captain Awesome's official sidekick. We'll call you Turbo: The Heroic Hamster, and you can use your Super Gnawing Power to—"

Panic filled Eugene's heart and backed up into his throat. Turbo was gone!

"Arrrrgh!" Eugene yelled. "Not again!"

Who could've done such a thing? Did Queen Stinkypants follow him to school?! Impossible! Her feet don't even reach the pedals on her Terror Tricycle. And he couldn't smell any of her stinky stinkiness in the air. This had to be the work of some new supermenace.

Eugene spotted a trail of cage shavings leading to the back of the room. *Good boy, Turbo!*, Eugene thought. *Leaving a trail so I can find you! What a smart little sidekick!*

The shavings led to the cubbies where the class kept their backpacks. The trail stopped at a pink backpack.

"There you are!" Ms. Beasley called out. "We're all outside for recess, Eugene."

"But-I-It's-Just-Um-Ah!" Eugene stammered.

"Go get some fresh air, sunshine, and monkey bars, kiddo."

Eugene sighed and trudged into the hall. Super Dude would never leave a man behind enemy

lines. Sure, Turbo was a hamster,
but Super Dude would never leave
a hamster behind either. Even to
go play on monkey bars.

Neither would Eugene.

"Hold on, little guy," Eugene
whispered, even though
Turbo couldn't hear
him. "I'll be back
for you.

I PROMISE. . . ."

CHAPTER 8

Captain Awesome Hatches an Awesome Plan

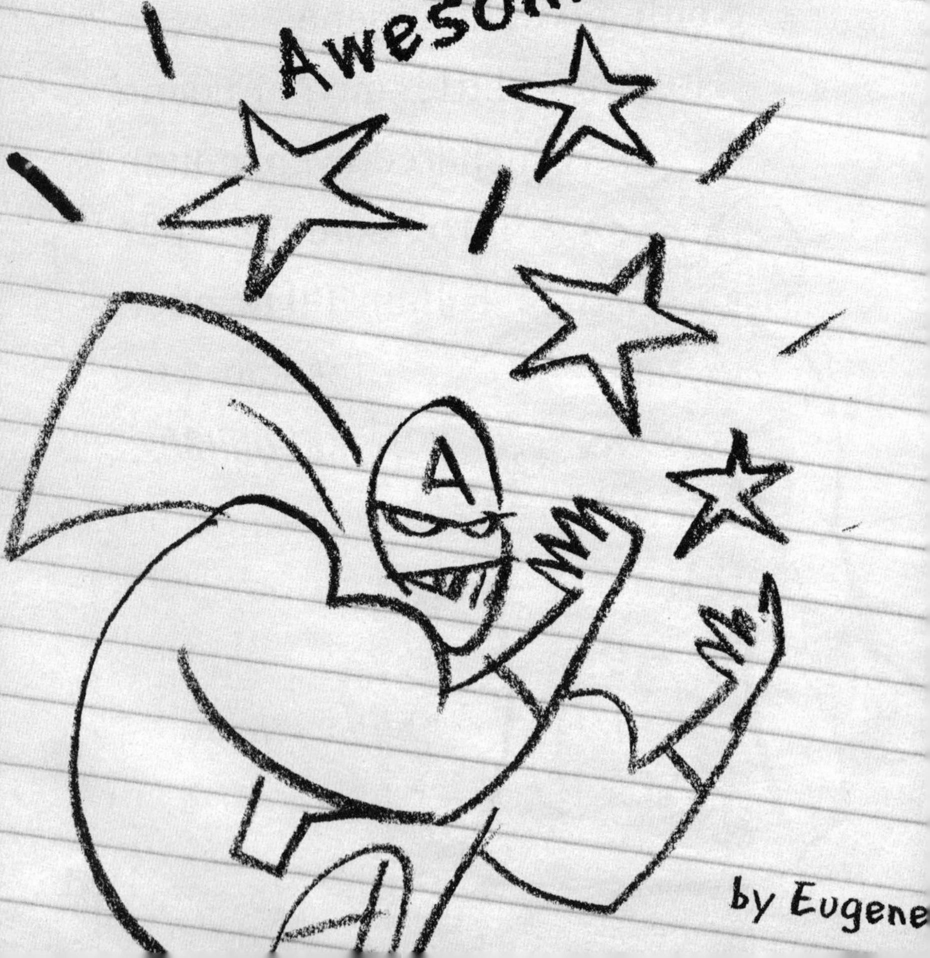

Kids screamed. They kicked balls, played games, and ran around like pretend airplanes in an imaginary sky.

Except for Eugene. He sat cross-legged near the tetherball courts. He had failed in his first mission for Ms. Beasley. Who would ever trust him with a small caged animal again? Not even the cafeteria's Mystery Meatloaf Surprise made him feel this sick. Then Meredith Mooney stuck her tongue out at him. He didn't feel like much of a hero now.

"Hey, there, Eugenio! Eugene!" Eugene was so lost in thought that he barely heard Charlie. "You look like your sister spilled gravy on your favorite issue of Super Dude."

"Worse, Charlie. Much worse. Turbo's been hamsternapped."

"No!" Charlie gasped.

"And I think Little Miss

Stinky—I mean Meredith did it."

"NO!" Charlie gasped even louder.

Eugene stopped talking so Charlie could catch his breath.

"We can't let her get away with it!" Charlie exclaimed. "The Fans of Super Dude Society won't stand for it!"

"The Fans of Super Dude Society?"

"I thought we needed a name for our club," Charlie said.

"We have a club?" Eugene asked.

"Sure! It's the 'Fans of Super Dude Society'! We friends gotta stick together."

Eugene smiled. Not because he was in a club called, awesomely enough, the Fans of Super Dude Society, or FsssDsss for short, but because Charlie had referred to him as a friend! **MI-TEE!**

Eugene stood up, suddenly filled with awesomeness once more . . . and was smacked in the head by the tetherball.

"OW!"

"Sorry!" Ryan Fitzpatrick said.

Eugene had a plan. Never sit next to the tetherball court again. Okay, Eugene had *two* plans, and the other was as cool as a Super Dude plan. "But I'm going to need *your* help after recess!" he said to Charlie.

"Anything for a fellow member of the FsssDsss!" Charlie replied.

CHAPTER 9

Captain Awesome Saves the Day and the Hamster

by Eugene

Ms. Beasley started class with geography. "Can anyone tell me the capital of France?" she asked.

That's when Eugene gave Charlie the thumbs-up.

"Help!"

"No, Charlie," she corrected. "It's Paris."

"No! No! No! Help!" Charlie repeated. "My desk's gone crazy!"

Charlie's desk rocked like a wild bull. His feet bounced the desk into Bernie Melnick's, which fell into Marlo Craven's and then into Evan Mason's.

"Charlie Thomas Jones!"

"I just can't . . . stop . . . it, Ms. Beasley!" Charlie gasped. "This is the . . . strongest, most . . .

powerful desk . . . I've ever . . . seen!"

While Charlie distracted the class, Eugene ran to his cubby and unzipped the secret compartment of his backpack. He took out his Captain Awesome suit, straightened on his cape, and got ready to save his hamster friend.

"Time to get MI-TEE!"

Eugene raced to the front of the class, his towel-cape fluttering behind him. He skidded to a stop before Ms. Beasley, who met him with a raised brow.

"Hold, citizen! For I, Captain Awesome, have something to say!"

Charlie's mouth dropped open. His desk stopped moving. The class sat in silence and waited for the caped hero of goodness's next words.

Captain Awesome spun and pointed a finger toward Turbo's cage. "Earlier today I found out that your class pet—the hamster known as Turbo—had disappeared!"

The class gasped in shock, and so did Ms. Beasley.

"Someone took our Turbo?" Ms. Beasley asked, a little surprised she was talking to a boy dressed in a superhero getup in the middle of her classroom.

Captain Awesome pointed to the trail of shavings that led from the cage to the backpack cubbies. "Gaze upon the trail of shavings! It goes right to the backpack with a pink ribbon! And we *all* know who wears a *pink* ribbon!"

"My Uncle Lewis!" Mike Flinch called out.

"No!" Captain Awesome continued. **"Meredith Mooney!"**

The students gasped again. Even Ms. Beasley was speechless for a moment. Meredith put her hands on her head, trying to hide the ribbons.

"Those are some serious accusations, Captain . . .

what was it again?" Ms. Beasley asked.

"Awesome, ma'am. Captain Awesome. As in 'Wow! He's AWESOME!'"

"You have no proof it was me, Captain

Grossface!" Meredith defended. "I'm not the only one who wears pink ribbons. How do you know it wasn't Mike's uncle Lewis?"

"Because I don't think Mike's uncle Lewis has a pink backpack!"

Captain Awesome looked quickly to Mike to make sure. Mike shook his head no.

Captain Awesome picked up the pink backpack at the end of the shavings trail. He read the name tag. "This pink backpack

with the pink ribbon has a name
tag that reads: 'Meredith Mooney.'
Let's see what's inside."

Meredith jumped from her
desk. "You can't do that! That's *my*
backpack! Ms. Beasley!"

"My. Me. Mine.
Mere-DITH," Captain

Awesome said and unzipped the backpack.

Turbo raced out and climbed onto Captain Awesome. "Just like Super Dude says: 'Danger is my middle name,'" Captain Awesome whispered to his furry sidekick.

Ms. Beasley turned to Meredith. "Well . . . ?"

"It's all true!" Meredith sniffed. "I took Turbo and hid him in my backpack. I wanted to be the one to take care of him, not Eugene. It was my turn, not his."

"Meredith . . . ," Ms. Beasley began calmly. "I didn't ask Eugene to watch Turbo to punish you. I just wanted to make Eugene feel welcome. It's not easy being some-place new, and sometimes it helps to know that there are people who care."

Captain Awesome tried to hide his smile. It looked like Ms. Beasley wasn't a brain-sucker after all.

Captain Awesome took Turbo in his hands and carried him back to his cage. "And now I, Captain Awesome, must leave, for there are other children with other missing class pets and stuff like that. Good-bye, children of Ms. Beasley's class. I'll be seeing you! Don't forget to brush your teeth!"

Captain Awesome raced out the door. Then a second later he raced back in.

"And feel free to give that kid Eugene all your desserts at lunch time!"

And just like that, Captain Awesome was gone.

Minutes later, Eugene came back into the classroom.

"So did I miss anything?" he asked with a smile.

CHAPTER 10

The End Is Right Here

by Eugene

"This was a pretty—*cough, cough*—awesome day," Charlie said as he and Eugene walked home after school. "Not everybody gets to rescue a hamster from the bad guys."

"If comic books teach us anything," Eugene said, "it's that Badness always loses to Goodness."

Eugene was put in charge of Turbo,

SUPER DUDE
THE SUPEREST DUDE OF ALL!
#902

REMEMBER, KIDS— BADNESS ALWAYS LOSES!

and Meredith lost recess for a week.

"Dude, you have no idea how cool it is that you're a superhero!" Charlie said, then carefully looked around. "Can I tell you a secret? I'm a superhero, too!"

Eugene was shocked. "No!"

"Yes!" Charlie said. "I'm the one and only Nacho Cheese Man! I have the power of canned cheese." Charlie pulled out a plastic bottle of canned cheese from his backpack. He popped the cap and blasted the letter C against a tree trunk.

"I knew you liked cheese,"

Eugene said. "But who knew it would give you superpowers!"

"I've been practicing," Charlie said. "You never know when you might need some cheese to

fight the forces of evil." Charlie held up a second can. "This one's taco-flavored to put a rumble in evil's tummy!"

"This is great news, Charlie! Two superheroes to fight Sunny-view's bad guys are way better than one!" Eugene said.

"Yeah! Let's form a superhero club," Charlie suggested.

"We'll need a name." Eugene thought for a moment. "Like the

SUNNYVIEW SUPERHERO SQUAD."

"I like it!" Charlie said.

"Together we shall defeat the forces of evil!" Eugene stood with his hand on his hips. "We'll find missing library books! Solve the riddles of the school's heating system! Figure out what Sudoku means!"

"Yeah! Now we need a slogan! And a theme song!"

"One thing at a time, Nacho Cheese Man, one thing at a time."

Together with Turbo, the boys headed home. Another day was ending.

Another day had been saved.

And Meredith? She was still stuck at school, cleaning out Turbo's cage.

THE

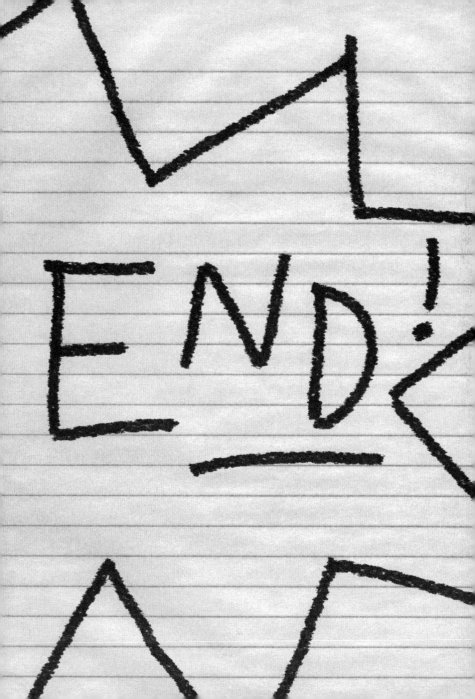

Table of Contents

CHAPTER I

The Slobbering Power
of Mr. Drools

By
Eugene

"**B**y the super MI-TEE force of Captain Awesome and the canned cheese power of Nacho Cheese Man, I call this Sunnyview Superhero Squad tree house sleepover meeting to order."

THUMP!

Eugene McGillicudy banged a wooden spoon against an empty shoebox. The Sunnyview Superhero Squad meeting had begun.

Sunnyview? Superhero? Squad?

That's right! Eugene and his best friend Charlie Thomas Jones were not just ordinary students at Sunnyview Elementary. They also had super secret super-hero identities.

Eugene was **Captain Awesome** and Charlie was **Nacho Cheese Man.**

122

Together, along with Captain Awesome's hamster sidekick (and the class pet), **Turbo**, they formed the Sunnyview Superhero Squad to protect the universe from bad guys.

"Hurry up," Charlie said. "The brownies are waiting!"

Brownies! Yum! The perfect superhero snack! thought Eugene. Evil doesn't stand a chance against chocolate fudge.

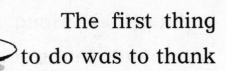

The first thing to do was to thank Eugene's mom, Betsy, for the homemade brownies and milk that she brought to the tree house. The next order of business was to eat them!

"Thanks, Mom," Eugene said, his mouth stuffed full of brownie.

"Thmph, Mmphs Mmmklldph," Charlie mumbled, trying not to dribble any on his Super Dude T-shirt.

"You're welcome, Charlie . . . I think," Eugene's mom said. Having delivered her sweet superhero treats, she climbed back down the ladder.

She knew that when it came to saving the world from the bad guys, it was always best for moms and dads to leave it to the experts: Captain Awesome and Nacho Cheese Man!

The Sunnyview Superhero Squad had one mission: **to stop the evily spread of evil in Sunnyview.** Their one mission, however, had three parts.

1. Be alert to evil.

2. Find evil.

3. Stop evil from eviling.

"I think we should add part number four: Eat more brownies!" Charlie quickly stuffed another brownie into his mouth.

"All those in favor of our mission—"

Charlie raised his hand. "Ambd meefing mrr mrownees?"

"Yes, Nacho Cheese Man. Including 'Eat more brownies,'" Eugene replied. "Those in favor, say the super word of the day!"

"MI-TEE!" Eugene and Charlie said at the same time. Even Turbo let out a little squeak.

Eugene banged the wooden spoon against the shoe box again. **_THUMP! THUMP! THUMP!_** It was time for the Squad's main non–evil-stopping activity (besides eating more brownies): reading the latest issue of Super Dude!

"Issue number four hundred twenty-nine!" Charlie cheered.

"Only the greatest thing since issue number four hundred twenty-eight!" Eugene declared.

Each member of the Sunnyview Superhero Squad . . . Wait. What's that you say? You've never heard of Super Dude? You're not a member of FsssDsss, the Friends of Super Dude Society, like Eugene and Charlie? You don't know about his TV show, toys, games, action figures, and more? Where do you live? The Moon?!

Super Dude is only the most

amazing superhero of all time. Just listen!

Eugene opened the comic. "Page one: Super Dude's archnemesis Trash Can't was back in Super City. 'I'm ready to crush Super Dude and trash his inner dudeness.'"

"Whoa. This is going to be the greatest issue ever!" Eugene could barely wait to turn the page!

And it was! Just when it looked like Super Dude would lose for sure and Trash Can't would litter his evil garbageness across the world,

Super Dude punched Trash Can't right in the recycling bin and dumped him on the curb in time for trash day.

Eugene turned the last page and closed the comic. He and Charlie sat in silence.

"That was the greatest thing I've ever read," Eugene finally said with a sigh, still in awe. "This is, without a doubt, my most favorite comic book . . . ever! No. Make that double-ever!"

"Whoa. The only thing I've *ever* double-evered was peanut-butter-fudge nachos with marshmallows. You know, the tiny ones?" Charlie said.

With the latest awesome issue of Super Dude completed, Eugene rubbed Turbo's furry head. "Good night, buddy."

"Good night, Turbo," Charlie said and clicked off his flashlight.

Soon both heroes were fast asleep and the tree house was filled with the squeak of Turbo's exercise

wheel as it spun round and round.

Then there was a **_BUMP!_**
Eugene opened one sleepy eye.

That's probably nothing.

Then he heard it again. **_THUMP!_**
His other eye snapped open.

That's something. My Captain Awesome Danger Sense is tingling!

Something was in the yard. Eugene sat up in his sleeping bag and listened. **_RATTLE!_**

Could it be?!

"GRRRRR! ROWL! SNARL!"

Yes, it was! His old furry enemy **Mr. Drools** had returned! Mr. Drools was the hairy four-legged monster from the Howling Paw Nebula whose drooly jaws

loved to chomp everything Eugene held most dear.

And worse, his evil Drool House was right next door to Eugene's home. Mr. Drools had turned the once normal house into his own "barkyard."

He's stolen three Frisbees, popped my soccer ball, eaten the cover off my baseball, and ripped up my kite like an old sock! What's he after this time?! Eugene wondered. Then he realized something awful. . . . *NOOOOOOOOO! NOT MY SUPER DUDE ISSUE No. 429!?*

Eugene jumped up without unzipping his sleeping bag. He hopped like the rare hopping cater-pillars of Mothonia in Super Dude

No. 97. He hopped on his flashlight, lost his balance, and fell to the wooden floor.

Eugene crawled from his sleeping bag.

Splinter!

"Ouch! Ouch! Ouch!"

Since superheroes can do anything, Eugene quickly pulled out the splinter. He felt around for his flashlight and clicked it on.

This was a nighttime job for Captain Awesome and Nacho Cheese Man!

"Wake up!" he whispered to

Charlie. "Mr. Drools is in his barkyard next door!"

Charlie shot out of his sleeping bag like he'd been stuck with a pin. He grabbed the emergency can of nacho cheese he kept under his pillow.

Eugene placed Turbo into the Turbomobile. They would need the power of two heroes and one sidekick to stop the barking, slobbery madness of Mr. Drools.

"Go chase your tail, Mr. Drools! You'll never get my comic book!"

Captain Awesome called down from the tree house. "Your slobber is useless on this night!"

"I must warn you now . . . ," Nacho Cheese Man called out. "I've got cheese!"

The trio of heroes climbed down from their tree house moon base and onto the cold surface of the Moon. . . .

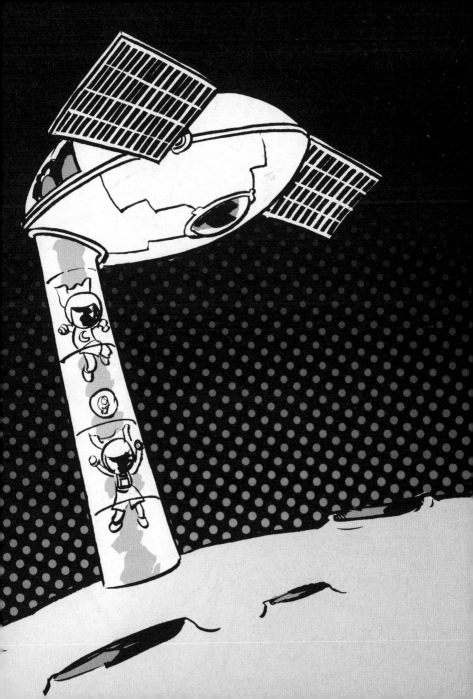

CHAPTER 2

Fighting Evil Is Messy

By Eugene

"What a mess!" Charlie said as he stood in the middle of Eugene's backyard the next morning. He picked up a can of cheese and shook it. Empty.

"That's just one of the many problems with evil." Eugene picked up an old banana peel and dropped it into the trash can. "It never picks up after itself."

Mr. Drools had gotten away. He escaped thanks to his Doggie Door of Droolness, but he'd return. The bad guys always do.

Eugene's mom smiled as the boys came into the house. "Here you go, boys. Super Dude-O's, the breakfast of the world's greatest superhero."

In many ways Eugene's mom

was a hero
too. She didn't wear a cape
or fight evil, but her ongoing battle
against cavities, late homework,
and tantrums was almost as important as saving the world. Almost.
Plus she always whipped up awesome breakfasts to make Eugene
superhero strong.

The two boys ate faster than

Sir Snacksalot who once challenged Super Dude to an eating contest. Super Dude won by eating fried okra.

After breakfast Charlie headed to his house down the street, and Eugene returned to his backyard. The moment he turned the corner, his nose was instantly filled with the stinky stink of stink!

"YUCK! THE STINKY STINK OF STINK!" Eugene gasped.

"GROSS!" Eugene held his nose.

Eugene didn't have to smell another stink bomb to know what was up.

It was **Queen Stinkypants** from Planet Baby! Her Dangerous Diaper of Doom was packed with stinky diaper awfulness.

"Gaa-baa-boo," she said in her alien baby language as she waddled across Eugene's backyard.

She hasn't seen me yet, Eugene thought.

Eugene knew she was up to something. Queen Stinkypants was always up to something.

She walked, fell, crawled, and waddled to the gate. So! She was the one who opened the secret passageway from Mr. Drools's

barkyard to the surface of the Moon. She wanted Mr. Drools to return for the Super Dude comic he didn't get last night.

"Well, not today! Not tonight! Never again, and never ever!" Eugene called out in his awesome Captain Awesome voice.

Eugene ripped off his shirt and revealed . . . that he'd forgotten to put on his Captain Awesome outfit underneath. Brrrr! Cold!

Eugene ran inside the house and grabbed his outfit from the laundry. "Gotta have it, Mom! Danger is all around me! Stinky danger!"

"Danger smells?" his mother asked, smiling.

"It does when it's stinky!" Eugene changed on the run. That meant he crashed into a hall door—**OUCH!**—bounced off a wall—**OOF!**—and then slid across the kitchen floor on his stomach.

WHEE!

Eugene flung open the screen door.

"Stop, villain!"

Queen Stinkypants turned to face him. "Glyxl?" she threatened.

Captain Awesome did an awesome jump onto the surface of the Moon. **MI-TEE!**

"Stop your eviling and please . . . take a bath!"

CHAPTER 3

The Missing Comic Book Caper

By Eugene

"Mom! Have you seen it?" Eugene screeched down the stairs.

"Seen what, dear?"

What? How could she not know the "what" I'm talking about? It's only the most important thing in forever!

Eugene was shocked. Was his

mother not aware of Super Dude? Did she not see the posters, the DVDs, the collectible action figures on her son's dresser?

Eugene's bestest, favoritist comic book in his whole collection was not in its special hiding spot in the box under his bed. **It was gone.**

Super Dude No. 429 was missing!

Did Mr. Drools sneak into Eugene's room, take Super Dude No. 429 in his giant paws of evil, and run away with it?

Panic began to hit Eugene. The thought was too horrible to imagine! All that drool all over Super Dude!

"And I double-evered that issue!"

He checked his bedroom floor. No muddy footprints. No bite marks on the door. No fleas hopping about on Eugene's pillow. No sign that Mr. Drools had made it inside Captain Awesome's secret headquarters.

But the comic book was gone. And someone had taken it. No one had been in his room except . . .

Aw, BARF! I showed my comic to Charlie when we were in the tree house. But no member of

the Sunnyview Superhero Squad would do anything bad . . . right?

Right?

Eugene slumped. He missed his comic book so much he was even thinking his best friend took it. That was the worst thought he had ever had . . . except for the one about the drool being all over Super Dude.

CHAPTER 4

Turbo Day

By Eugene

"Turbo! Turbo! Turbo!"

The class chanted the name of their pet hamster. It was Thursday and that meant it was Turbo Day. As Turbo's caretaker, Eugene made sure to get him to school early.

In Ms. Beasley's second-grade classroom, Turbo Day meant a celebration of everything Turbo.

You only need two things to have Turbo Day:

1) Turbo

2) A Day

If there's one thing that would cheer up Eugene, it was Turbo Day. And it would give him a chance to check Charlie's cubby for the missing comic book.

Y'know. Just in case.

"Turbo! Turbo! Turbo! Who's the hamster on the go? It's Turbo!" The class sang a special cheer written just for Turbo.

The class was distracted by Turbo's cuteness and good hamster manners. Now was Eugene's chance! He wandered to the back of the room. No one was looking.

No Super Dude comic. But he did find a few half-empty cans of cheese.

If Charlie was the thief, he was more clever than Commander Nylon, who kept stealing Super Dude's socks while he was sleeping and used them to stitch a humongous sock monster.

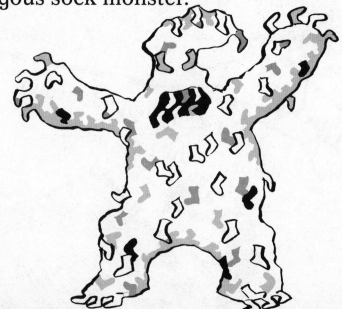

Eugene snuck back to the circle just in time for the Turbo game. Turbo rolled around the floor in his plastic ball showing off his athletic skills.

Awesome. Look at him go! What a good little sidekick! Eugene proudly thought.

The class squealed and cheered with delight. Turbo Day was a success!

"Turbo Force . . . now!" Eugene called out to Turbo.

Everyone will be impressed when Turbo rolls right to me just like he always does. Eugene smiled at the thought.

Turbo rolled . . . and rolled . . . and rolled past Eugene.

Right.

Past.

Eugene.

WHAT?! Where's he going?

Turbo rolled to . . .

Charlie? ***GAHHH!*** This is worse than the time that Super Squirrel bit Super Dude's super finger when Super Dude fed him that Super Acorn from the Super Oak Tree!

"Charlie?" Eugene called out. "Why did Turbo roll right to you?"

Charlie shrugged. "I don't know, but that was cool, huh?" Charlie patted the top of the hamster ball and carried it over to Turbo's cage.

What's going on here? My favorite comic book in forever is missing and now my faithful side-kick has Turbo Forced to somebody else?

Eugene quickly looked around the classroom to see if anyone was using a mind-control hat. There could be no other explanation. But there was no one with a mind-control hat. Eugene realized there *must* be another explanation.

There must be. . . .

CHAPTER 5

The Evilest Field Trip of All

By
Eugene

"Okay, everyone," Ms. Beasley called out. "Let's get moving!"

The best thing about school that isn't Turbo Day is a class field trip. Eugene couldn't wait. If anything could take his mind off his missing comic, it would be a trip to the zoo. He loved field trips. If you asked Eugene what his favorite class was in school, his answer would be field trip.

His *second* favorite class?

"Another field trip."

And a trip to the zoo would also give Eugene a chance to see if there was any crime or bad stuff happening in Sunnyview. Plus he'd see some pretty cool animals.

As his classmates filed out of the classroom, Eugene pretended to tie his shoelace. After the class was empty, he scampered to Charlie's desk and searched through his things. Books. Pencils. A ruler. Cans of cheese. But still no sign of Super Dude No. 429.

Maybe I'm wrong about Charlie. But who else could've taken my comic?

"Eugene? Are you coming?" Ms. Beasley asked, poking her head back into the classroom.

"Coming!" Eugene raced for the door. He'd be the last one on the bus, but that was no problem.

Charlie would save a seat for him like he always did.

You can always count on a superhero best friend.

Eugene raced up the steps and onto the bus. He now felt silly for thinking his best friend, Charlie, had taken his comic book. He couldn't wait to sit next to him for the long ride to the zoo.

And then the world turned upside down! Eugene's mouth hit the floor! He saw the most horrible thing he could ever possibly see except for that time his dad gave him a haircut.

Meredith Mooney was sitting next to Charlie. Not Eugene . . . Meredith. The awful "ME . . . MY . . . MEREDITH!"

ARGH!

"Hey, Charlie!" Eugene said. "I thought you were saving me a seat?"

"I got here first." Meredith smiled.

"Sorry, Eugene," Charlie said. "She did call 'firsties.'"

DOUBLE *ARGH!* What kind of person steals a seat on a bus? And what kind of a best friend lets a seat stealer call "firsties"?!

Seat-stealing is just the kind of thing a supervillain does when they're not trying to crush the world or steal radioactive waste from the Moon!

This was not Meredith Mooney, the girl who always wore pink ribbons in her hair. This was **Little Miss Stinky Pinky**, the sworn enemy of Captain Awesome, and no friend to his side-kick, Turbo, either. She had once hamsternapped him. Nacho Cheese Man knew she was bad, even if she did wear pink ribbons in her hair. But what was her evil plan?

Villains like Little Miss Stinky Pinky were always up to no good!

Maybe she was trying to get information out of Charlie. Or WORSE! WORSER THAN WORSE! Maybe she was trying to crush the Sunnyview Superhero Squad? Evil hates best friend superheroes!

"There's a seat up here, Eugene," Ms. Beasley called out and patted the empty seat next to her.

Sit next to the teacher on a field trip? **BARF!**

That's even worse than sitting next to your sister or getting cheek-pinched by wrinkly old Aunt Matilda!

What kind of Superhero Squad member is Nacho Cheese Man? Eugene wondered as he made the long, doomed journey to the seat next to Ms. Beasley. If he can't be counted on to battle all supervillains calling "firsties," what'll he do when a supervillain blasts the Earth with melted butter? *Nacho*

Cheese Man is no longer on the side of goodness and hamsters. He did steal my comic, I'll bet!

It was time now for Captain Awesome to confront a new, cheesy evil!

"You might not be able to stand up against bus seat firsties," Eugene said quietly. **"But keep your cheesy hands off my comic books!"**

CHAPTER 6

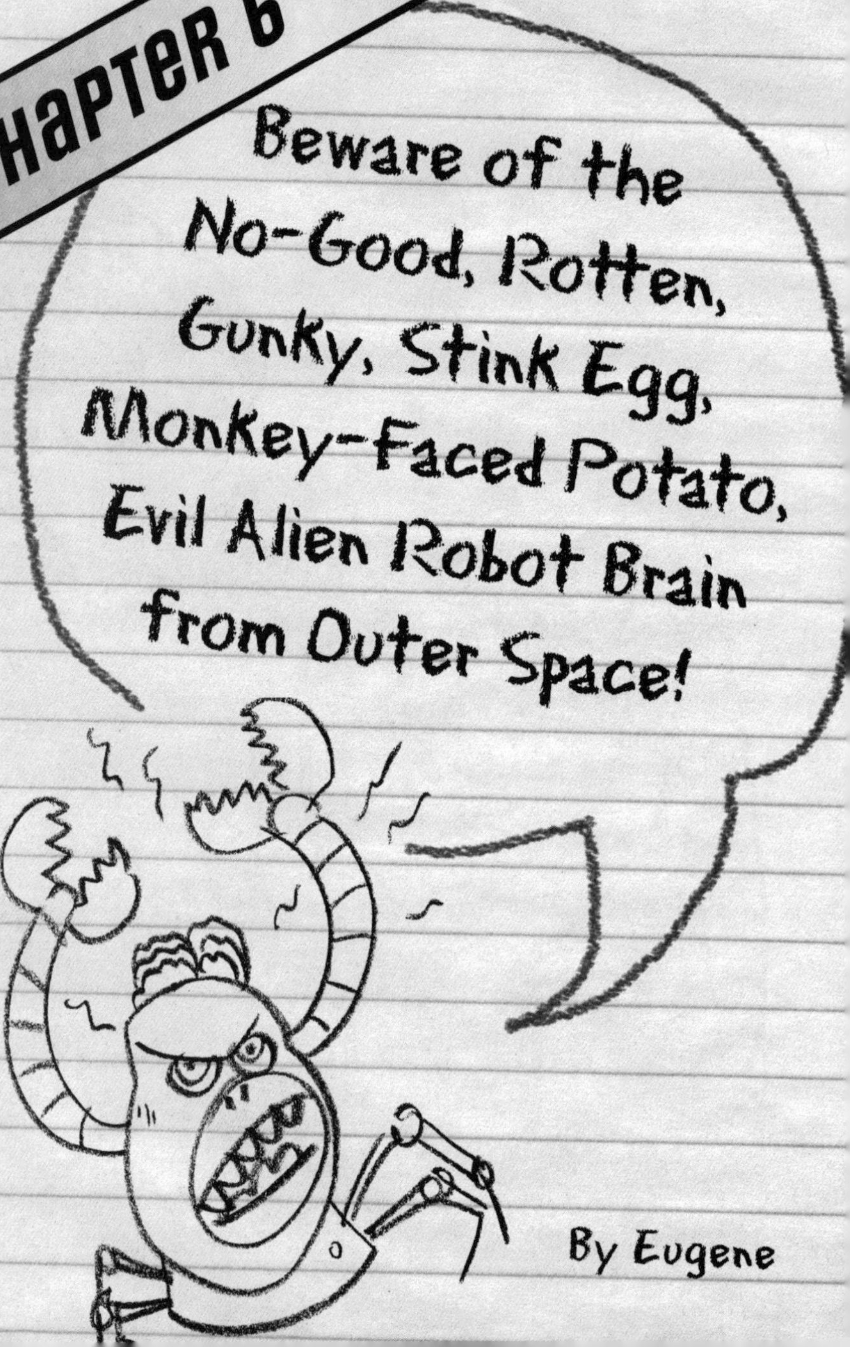
Beware of the No-Good, Rotten, Gunky, Stink Egg, Monkey-Faced Potato, Evil Alien Robot Brain from Outer Space!
By Eugene

Charlie rocked back and forth on his swing, trying to move. He wobbled, weebled and wobbled, then wobbled some more. No luck. He wasn't going anywhere. The thing about swings is, if you can't get going on your own, then it's really just like sitting in a chair with chains.

"It's your turn to push," Charlie finally said to

Eugene, who sat on the swing next to him.

Eugene didn't reply. He just scrunched his face up like he was pretending to be a prune.

"Eugene? It's your turn to—"

"NO WAY!" The words just exploded from Eugene's mouth.

Eugene jumped from his swing, looking more scrunchy and prune-faced than ever before and stomped to Charlie.

"Listen! CAPTAIN AWESOME is the leader of the Sunnyview Superhero Squad, NOT Nacho

Cheese Head!"

"Nacho Cheese *Man*," Charlie corrected, a little annoyed.

"And since CAPTAIN AWE-SOME is the leader of the Superhero Squad and NOT Nacho Bologna Head, you should be pushing *me* on the swings!" Eugene continued.

Now it was Charlie's turn to be quiet. He didn't know what to say or why Eugene was acting like he was. Then it hit him! Aliens stole his best friend's brain, stuck it in

a jar, and replaced it with an evil alien robot brain!

Charlie leaped from his swing! "Don't worry, Captain Awesome!" He used his heroic Nacho Cheese Man voice. "I'll save your brain!"

"*And* I know *you* stole my most favorite, best Super Dude comic book ever!"

"I did not!" Charlie said, defending himself.

"Did so! Issue number four hundred twenty-nine! You were there when I double-evered it!" Eugene said. "And you teamed up with the worstest, most evil, and pinkest supervillain in the whole biggest universe to do it: Little Miss Stinky Pinky!" *Gross!*

"You . . . you don't really mean that?" Charlie was stunned.

"I mean it like my mom does when she says 'eat your vege-tables or you won't get any dessert,'" Eugene growled.

Charlie's stomach twisted into knots and he felt sick—and not just because Eugene was talking about vegetables. "I was wrong," Charlie began. "Aliens didn't switch your brain with an evil alien robot brain . . . they switched it with a **NO-GOOD, ROTTEN, GUNKY, STINK EGG, MONKEY-FACED POTATO, EVIL ALIEN ROBOT BRAIN!**"

Charlie stomped off, then turned around. "And I never stole your stupid comic book!"Charlie stomped

off, then turned around again. "And
I quit the Superhero Squad!"

Charlie stomped off, but this
time, there was no more turning
around.

Eugene plopped back onto the
swing and crossed his arms.
He was angrier
than the time
Queen Stinkypants
flushed his Super Dude
action figure down the toilet. And
in fact Eugene would've been a lot
more angry . . . if he wasn't so sad.

CHAPTER 7

I Don't Feel Like Dessert.

By Eugene

Eugene sat at the table and stared at his vegetables. He rolled the peas to one side of his plate then rolled them behind the mashed potatoes so he wouldn't have to look at them. Eugene's mom made peas a lot. Sometimes she steamed them. Sometimes she boiled them. Sometimes she added butter. Sometimes she added tiny little onions. But no matter how she tried to disguise the little green things, they were still icky peas! **_BLECH!_**

Eugene lifted his mashed potatoes with his spoon and mushed them over the peas.

"Eat your vegetables or you won't get any dessert," his mom reminded him.

Eugene sighed. He didn't feel like eating anything anyway, including dessert.

Eugene's mom touched her son's hand. "You seem upset, Eugene. Is something wrong?"

Eugene shrugged and mumbled something that sounded like "Dere's muffin gong."

"I know what might cheer you up," his mom continued. "What if we asked Charlie's mom if Charlie can

come over this Friday for another sleepover?"

"Charlie's not my best friend! He's not even my *worst* friend! I'd rather have a sleepover with Queen Stinkypants than Charlie because at least I already know Queen Stinkypants is going to try to shoot me into space in a giant diaper, so it won't be a surprise when she does!"

Eugene raced from the table and ran to his room.

His mom and dad sat at the

table in shocked silence. Then Eugene's dad, Ned, asked, "Wait. Who's Queen Stinkypants?"

"I really think that one of us should go see what's up with him," Eugene's mom said.

"I'll go." Eugene's dad quickly got up from his seat. He hoped that, by the time he came back to the dinner table, his wife would've already thrown away the icky peas he'd hidden under the roast beef on his plate.

CHAPTER 8

Who's the Bad Guy Now?

By Eugene

Eugene's dad knocked on the door. Eugene covered his head with a pillow and mumbled, "Come in."

His dad sat on the bed. "Are you okay, son?" Eugene's dad felt a bit strange talking to a pillow. "Did something happen with Charlie?"

"Everything went wrong with Charlie!" Eugene blurted, throwing the pillow off his face. "Turbo rolled to Charlie and not me when I called 'Turbo Force,' then Charlie let

Meredith Mooney sit next to him on the bus just 'cause she called 'firsties,' and he wanted me to push him on the swing just 'cause it was my turn to push, and most of all he stole my favoritest double-evered

Super Dude number four hundred twenty-nine comic!" Eugene took a deep breath. Saying all those words at once made his face turn really red.

Eugene's dad thought about his son's problems very carefully, mostly because he had no idea what "Turbo Force," "firsties," and "double-evered" even meant, but also because he loved Eugene and didn't want to mess things up even more. Luckily, Eugene's dad knew one way he could help.

"Eugene, I don't think Charlie

stole your Super Dude comic. . . ."

"How would you know that unless you had X-ray vision or something?" Eugene paused for a moment, then asked hopefully, "*Do you have X-ray vision?*"

"No, son, but I do have this. . . ."

Eugene's dad pulled out the missing copy of Super Dude No. 429. Eugene practically fell out of his bed. How did his *dad* get his Super Dude comic!? Was *he* the one who took the comic from Eugene's room!? But *why*?! Then it hit Eugene! Aliens stole his dad's

brain, stuck it in a jar, and replaced
it with an evil alien robot brain!

Eugene leaped from his bed!
"Don't you worry, Dad! Captain
Awesome will save your brain!"

"My brain is fine. Although . . .
I do get a little headache sometimes

when I see your mom's made more peas for dinner. . . ."

"But why did you take my comic?" If aliens didn't steal his dad's brain . . . well, Eugene was very confused.

"I didn't take it. I found it in Molly's baby doll stroller. And I think she took it because she wanted to play with you. She wanted to do something you liked to do."

She wanted to play *with me?* Eugene thought. "When I saw her in the backyard, I kinda called her a 'bad guy' and told her to not open the doorway to the barkyard," Eugene confessed, feeling rotten.

"Molly was going to open the doorway ... to the, oh ... back-yard? That *is* pretty serious stuff." Eugene's dad put an arm around his son. The boy stared quietly at the Super Dude comic. "Eugene, do you know what makes Super Dude a *super*hero? It's not the costume or the

superpowers, it's because, when someone needs help, Super Dude does *everything* he can to help them, no matter *who* they are. He treats everyone with kindness and respect—except for the bad guys, of course. And that makes him someone the rest of us can look up to and admire . . . just like Molly does to you, her big brother."

The last words made Eugene have a terrible thought—yes, even more terrible than Super Dude covered in drool. He hadn't been very nice to his little sister, and if she was the one who took his Super Dude comic, then he had been pretty rotten to Charlie as well.

The thought was really hard for Eugene to swallow, even harder than his mom's icky peas. Maybe it was Captain Awesome who was acting like the "bad guy" after all.

CHAPTER 9

Something Better Than Pizza

By Eugene

The next day at school was Friday.

Pizza Friday!

Pizza Fridays are the most awesome day of the week because, in case you couldn't guess by the name, they served pizza in the cafeteria. Eugene loved it . . . much more than Mystery Meat Mondays.

Actually, Eugene loved almost anything more than Mystery Meat Mondays.

But this Friday, Eugene wasn't very excited about much—even pizza. He took a bite of the cheesy triangle and sighed. Usually, he and Charlie would see who could make the longest cheese string from their mouths to the pizza slice, but making cheese strings wasn't much fun sitting alone.

Charlie was sitting across the cafeteria. He wasn't making cheese strings, either. Eugene picked up

his lunch tray and headed over. Eugene had a lot to say. There was so much to explain, but he left it all up to one word:

"Sorry."

Charlie shrugged and ate his pizza.

Eugene continued. "Captain Awesome didn't—I mean *I* didn't treat you very well and I'm sorry. Will you please come back to the Sunnyview Superhero Squad?"

"Because the safety of the universe kinda depends on it?" Charlie asked.

"No," Eugene replied. "Because you're my best friend."

Charlie smiled. He was about to say something, but made a cheese string instead. "I bet you can't beat that one!"

Eugene bit his pizza. A gooey cheesy cheese string stretched from his mouth to the pizza slice.

The string broke and flopped over Eugene's chin.

"MI-TEE!" Eugene and Charlie said at the same time.

The two boys laughed and their happiness washed away any bad feelings over their fight.

So bad guys beware! Nacho Cheese Man and Captain Awesome were back. The Sunnyview Superhero Squad was together again!

And just in time for a sleepover
on Friday night.

CHAPTER 10

The Stink of Friendship

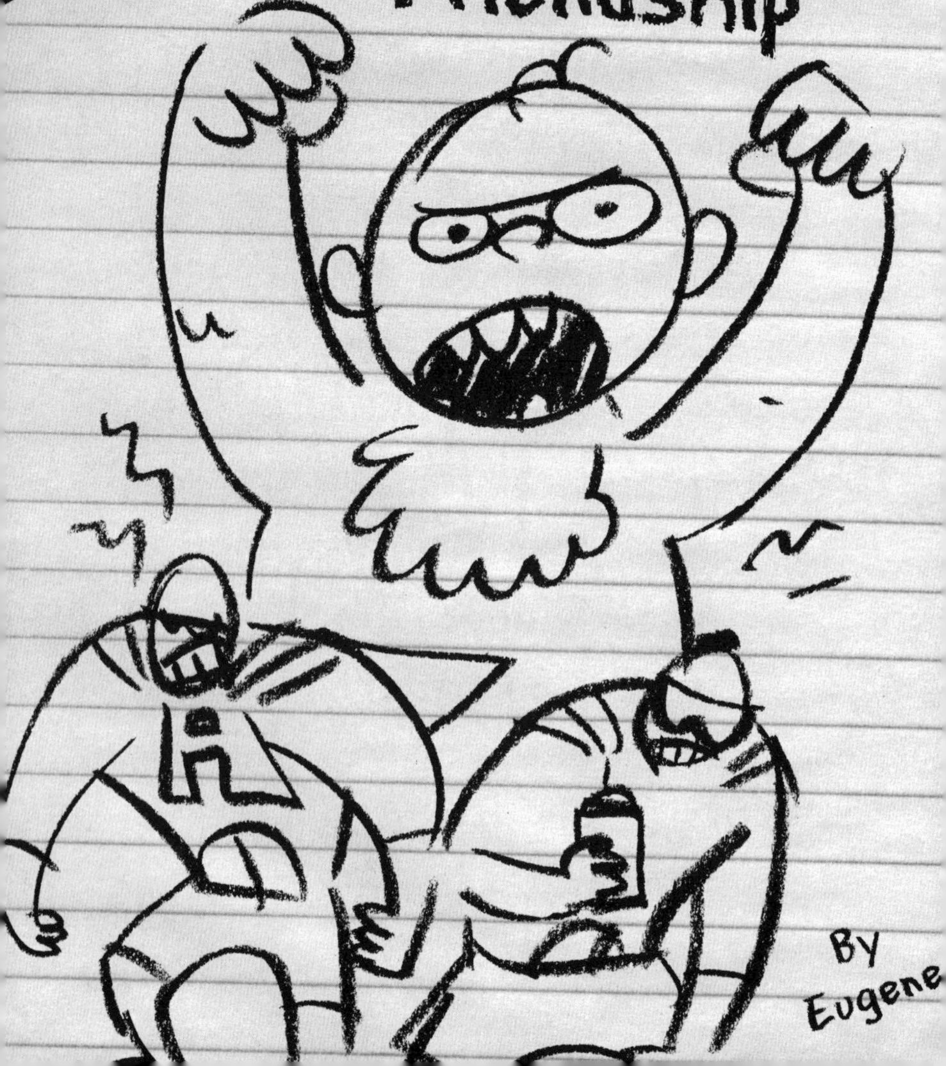

The next morning Eugene and Charlie both woke with a start. **"HOOOOWWWWWWL!"**

"Charlie! Mr. Drools is back!" Eugene gasped and quickly reached under his pillow to make sure Super Dude No. 429 was still there.

"I'm all cheesed up and ready to go!" Charlie whipped out two cans of cheese and popped the tops.

ZIP! ZIP!

In a flash the boys pulled out their superhero outfits, and a moment later, Captain Awesome, Nacho Cheese Man, and Turbo—in his plastic hamster ball, the Turbomobile—climbed down the ladder to do battle with the droolicious Mr. Drools!

They jumped off the ladder and onto the surface of the moon, only to be met by the shocking sounds of gibberish!

"Gah-gwarr-goo-gee! *GAAAH!*"

"Oh no!" Nacho Cheese Man cried out, holding his canned cheese even tighter. "It's Queen Stinky-pants!"

Eugene was about to unleash some awesome Captain Awesome awesomeness on his archenemy, but then he remembered what his dad had said.

"I . . . I think she just wants to play with us—I mean, fight evil with us," Captain Awesome said, just in time to stop Nacho Cheese

Man from launching his three-cheese attack. "We can always use some extra hero-power to defeat Mr. Drools!"

Queen Stinkypants was going to help them? Nacho Cheese Man was confused for a second. Then he realized Super Dude's famous Rule 42:

Sometimes evil teams up with goodness to fight a bigger evil.

Maybe it was like that with Mr. Drools and Queen Stinkypants. After all, the slobbering menace did gobble up the queen's favorite

Stinkdoll just last week.

Captain Awesome stuck out a hand to Queen Stinkypants and asked, "Do you want to help us?"

"Gwaaa-ha-ha-ha-heee-giggle-giggle!" Queen Stinkypants laughed with joy and she hugged Captain-Awesome's leg.

"No hugging." The Captain blushed and quickly unpeeled her. **"HOOOOWWWWWWL!"**

"Come on, heroes! Let's put Mr. Drools back in the doghouse!" Captain Awesome called out and led the charge.

There was a strange smile on Queen Stinkypants's face as the three heroes rushed into battle. There was an even stranger

smell coming from her diaper.
Captain Awesome knew he might
not be able to trust her forever,
but at least on this day, they were

three heroes fighting side by side against . . . **THE DREADED MR. DROOLS AND HIS PAWS OF DESTRUCTION—** and Eugene wouldn't have it any other way.

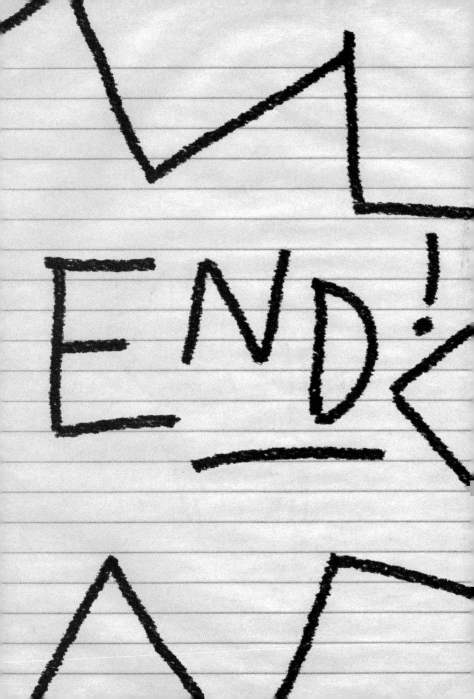

Captain Awesome

and the New Kid

Table of Contents

"RUN!"

Captain Awesome grabbed the Frisbee and raced for his life!

"We're not going to make it!" Nacho Cheese Man shouted, an empty can of cheese in his hand.

ROWWWWWL!

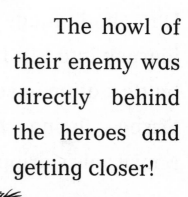

The howl of their enemy was directly behind the heroes and getting closer!

The Danger-Stopping Dynamic Duo had made the dangerous journey into Mr. Drools's Dog Star battle station to save their precious Frisbee being held captive in Mr. Drools's drippy, droolish jaws.

What's that? you say. You've never heard of **Mr. Drools?** He's only the most slobberingest monster from the Howling Paw Nebula! He wakes up neighborhoods around the galaxy with his barking, his Drool of Destruction, and his taste for Frisbees.

What's that? you say again. Who are **Captain Awesome** and **Nacho Cheese Man?!**

Only the two most awesomest heroes not named Super Dude.

Super Dude just happened to be *the* most awesome superhero in Eugene's comic book collection.

Eugene McGillicudy and his best friend, Charlie Thomas Jones, were not just ordinary students at Sunnyview Elementary. They also had supersecret superhero identities: Eugene was Captain Awesome and Charlie was Nacho Cheese Man.

Along with Captain Awesome's hamster sidekick, Turbo, together

they formed the Sunnyview Superhero Squad to protect the universe from bad guys.

Especially drooling space dogs.

Captain Awesome and Nacho Cheese Man had landed the

Awesome Rocket on Mr. Drools's dreaded Dog Star—a grrrnormous battle station, shaped like a dog's head—that flew around the uni-verse barking at helpless planets.

Boarding the Dog Star was the start of a three-part mission to save Eugene's favorite Frisbee.

The three parts were:

1. find the Frisbee

2. rescue the Frisbee, and

3. do not get drooled on by Mr. Drools! GROSS!

"GRRRRR!" Mr. Drools growled, drool squirting from his clenched teeth.

DOUBLE YUCK!

"Let's go!" shouted Captain Awesome, using his superspeed power to run through the long hallway of the Dog Star and nearly stepped on something lumpy. A scary thought jumped into Captain Awesome's head.

"Oh no! We're right in the middle of a Doggy Doo-Doo Minefield!" he shouted out to Nacho Cheese Man.

ICK!

A Doggy Doo-Doo Minefield was a scary *and* icky thought. Mr. Drools's Dog Star was full of traps! Very smelly traps . . .

"I'll stop the monster!" shouted Nacho Cheese Man. He grabbed a new can of power cheese from

his Cheese Bag so he could aim it at Mr. Drools.

PFSZZT!

Cheese blasted Nacho Cheese Man right in the face!

"Aargh!" he cried out. "I'm cheesed!"

Nacho Cheese Man had forgotten the first rule of the power of canned cheese: Point the can away from you.

"Mmmmm. It's yummy though!"

But it was not a time for snacks, no matter how yummy. Mr. Drools was within slobber range of the Frisbee. There was only one thing Captain Awesome could do.

WHIZZZ!

Captain Awesome threw the Frisbee to Nacho Cheese Man. Unfortunately, Nacho Cheese Man's face was still covered in gooey cheese. The Frisbee sailed over his head and Mr. Drools took off after it.

"The Frisbeeeeeeee!" cried out Captain Awesome.

"I'm on it!"

Nacho Cheese Man had his own Plan B: a Squeaky Dinky Squeezo. He pulled the doggie toy from his Cheese Bag and said the one word that no inhabitant of the Howling Paw Nebula could ever resist:

"FETCH!"

The Squeaky Dinky Squeezo worked! Mr. Drools took off after it.

"Good thinking, Nacho Cheese Man!" Captain Awesome exhaled. He was relieved.

"I learned from the best,"Nacho Cheese Man said, looking at his Super Dude watch. Super Dude had faced a similar situation in Super Dude No. 48 with The Kitty Litterer, The Cat That Littered. Super Dude had defeated her by using a giant ball of string.

While Mr. Drools dribbled his evil spittle on poor Squeaky Dinky, Captain Awesome grabbed the Frisbee and ran with Nacho Cheese Man toward the Dog Star airlock.

"MI-TEE!" Captain Awesome cried out and hopped onto his MI-TEE Mobile rocket bike and blasted away from the Dog Star. Nacho Cheese Man followed on his own rocket bike, The Cheesy Rider.

"Cheesy-Yoooo!" he cried as he took off.

But fast on their trail was
Mr. Drools, barking and drooling
as he chased after the boys.

Time for the Boomway!

They turned their rocket bikes
onto the Boomway, the outer

space bike path. Captain Awesome pushed the solar-drive button on his handlebars and launched the MI-TEE Mobile and The Cheesy Rider into the vastness of space.

They were sure to lose Mr. Drools in the King Crab Nebula, just past the Lobsteroid Belt. . . .

CHAPTER 2

The Neighbors Are Alien Spies

By Eugene

Eugene and Charlie pedaled their bikes around the block. Most kids would just call it bike riding, but to the members of the Sunnyview Superhero Squad, they were "on patrol."

Evil could lurk anywhere and around any corner. Even in a mailbox! If it was small evil, that is.

The boys turned the corner and Eugene slammed on his brakes. Unfortunately, he stopped too soon, flipped over the handlebars, and landed in a big pile of leaves.

"YAAAAAAAAAAAAA!"

"What is it, Eugene?" Charlie said.

"Leaves," Eugene said, holding up a maple leaf. "And a moving van."

Eugene pointed down their street to the end of the cul-de-sac. A moving van was parked in front of the red brick house.

"Maybe they have a kid our age," Charlie said.

"Yeah . . . maybe . . . ," Eugene started. "Or maybe it's a house full of aliens, or spies, or . . ."

"ALIEN SPIES!" The two boys shouted out in unison.

Sensing danger, they jumped into the bushes to hide!

"OUCH! PRICKLES!"

Eugene and Charlie jumped back out and hid behind the pile of leaves Eugene had crashed into.

"Do you think they're from a galaxy far, far away?" Charlie asked.

"Aren't all aliens from far away?" Eugene replied.

"What do you think they want?"

Eugene knew *exactly* what they wanted. "Our Super Dude comic books, that's what. Let's get a closer look," he whispered.

"Do you think they have two or four antennae sticking out of their heads?" Charlie was filled with fear and excitement. Antennae sticking out of aliens' heads will do that to a person.

Eugene snuck up the ramp and peeked into the moving van.

"What's inside?" Charlie whispered. "Danger?"

"Furniture."

"Alien spy furniture?"

"Only if alien spies ride bikes," Eugene whispered back.

"Looks like a human bike to me," Charlie said, joining Eugene in the van.

Everything seemed so . . .

NORMAL.

Maybe the aliens are trying to trick the Superhero Squad by pretending to be good guys who "come in peace!" Eugene thought.

"That's a really nice bike, isn't

it?" a mysterious voice asked. An alien spy stood in the doorway, blocking their escape. Eugene and Charlie were cut off!

We're trapped! I fell for the oldest trick in the book: alien spies pretending to be friendly new neighbors who distract me with cool bikes! thought Eugene.

"They don't come in peace, Charlie!" Eugene called out. "They're here to tear us to pieces!"

This alien spy would be no match for Captain Awesome and Nacho Cheese Man!

CHAPTER 3

It's New Kid Monday!

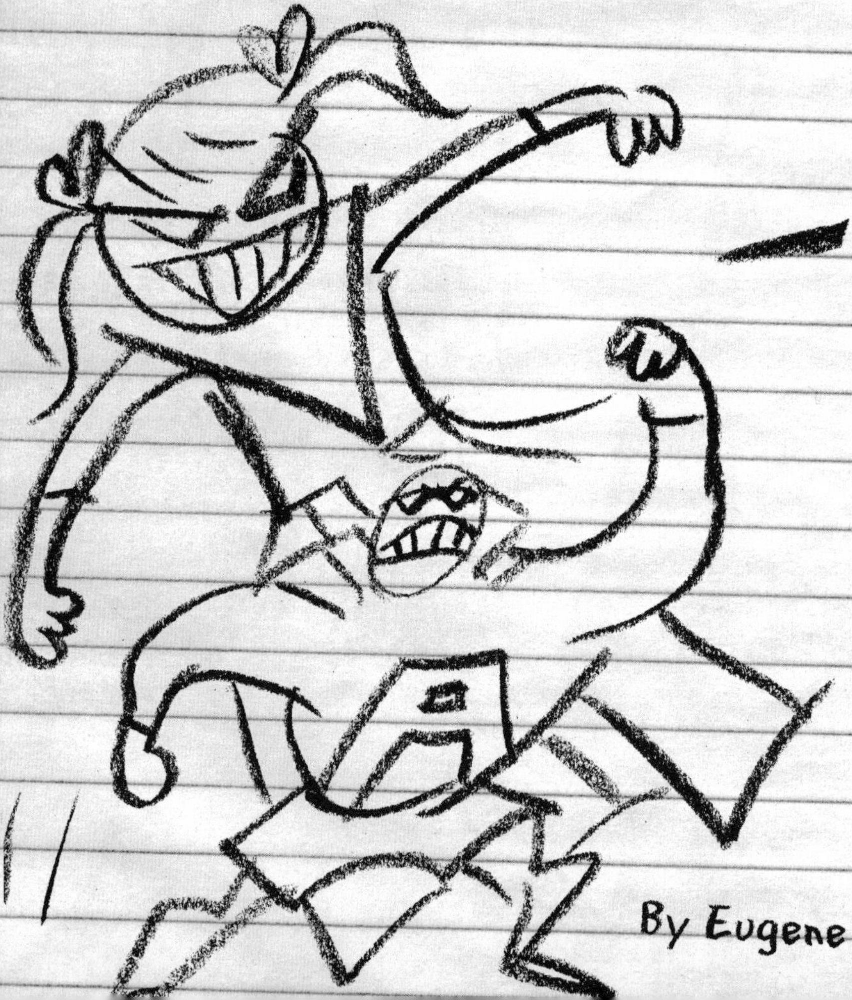

By Eugene

"**C**lass, we have a surprise today," Ms. Beasley said.

It was Monday, which meant Charlie and Eugene were back at school, their superhero uniforms secretly stuffed into their backpacks.

Eugene's eyes lit up when his teacher said "surprise."

What could it be? Pizza Friday is moving to Mondays? We're being sent home early?

Ms. Beasley continued, "Class, say hello to your new classmate Sally Williams."

Everyone was quiet. Even Turbo stopped spinning on his squeaky exercise wheel. The kids stretched their necks like human giraffes to see . . . nothing.

No one was in the doorway.

"WOW! Look! Sally's invisible!" Charlie cried out.

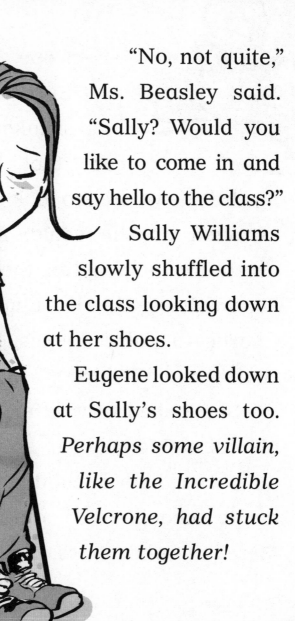

"No, not quite," Ms. Beasley said. "Sally? Would you like to come in and say hello to the class?"

Sally Williams slowly shuffled into the class looking down at her shoes.

Eugene looked down at Sally's shoes too. *Perhaps some villain, like the Incredible Velcrone, had stuck them together!*

Nope.

But her high-top sneakers were so cool that Eugene figured she wanted to look at them as often as she could. Besides, except for the ponytail, the rest of her was dressed just like Eugene and Charlie—a pair of jeans, blue of course, and a T-shirt.

She looked very different from Meredith Mooney. If the color pink ever had a child and sent her to school, she'd look just like Meredith—pink dress, pink socks,

pink shoes, and so many pink ribbons stuck in her hair that it looked like pink meteors had crashed into it.

"Class, let's all say a warm Sunnyview hi to Sally," Ms. Beasley said.

"Hiii, Sal-ly!" the class repeated together.

"Hi," Sally replied, still staring at her shoes, like she was trying to melt them with heat vision.

"Nice shoes," Meredith Mooney said. "For a boy. Is your name Sally Williams . . . or William Sally? That shirt looks like something my brother would wear. Actually, even *he* dresses

better than that. And everyone knows that boys have cooties."

Some of the class giggled.

Hearing the giggles made Meredith continue. "That makes you . . . the COOTIE QUEEN!"

The class roared with laughter, except for Eugene and Charlie. Eugene knew what it was like to be the new kid, and Charlie was too busy counting his cans of spray cheese.

"Meredith Mooney!" Ms. Beasley snapped.

Sally's face turned as red as the pickled beets in the cafeteria. She ran past Meredith's desk to an empty seat in the back of the class-room.

Eugene did what heroes do when they see or hear something wrong: HE spoke up.

"Hey! Be quiet! My! Me! Mine! Mere-DITH!" Eugene said. "Every-one knows that the *only* people with

cooties are girls
who wear the
barfy color pink
that's pink like the
color of barf."

The tide shifted and the class started to laugh at Meredith and chant, "Pink is barf! Barf is pink! Pink is barf that makes you stink!"

MI-TEE! Eugene thought. Victory was his! There was no way Meredith could have a comeback for pink barf!

Meredith stuck out her tongue at Eugene.

The ol' Tongue-Stick-Out!? Is that the best she could do? Eugene proudly thought.

"Thank you," Sally whispered so quietly Eugene thought his ears had been stolen.

Eugene whispered, "You're welcome," but Sally was already doodling in her notebook. Eugene sat in his chair, satisfied at his pink, barfy defeat of Meredith and then . . .

WAIT!

Oh . . .

NO!

GROSS!

Eugene felt something crawl up his arm.

He! Had! **COOTIES!**

It was all part of Meredith's evil cootie plan, for in reality, Meredith Mooney was much more than an annoying little girl who wore too much pink. She was really Captain Awesome's enemy, Little Miss Stinky Pinky!

Even Charlie was scratching the top of his head. He had cooties too!

I say NAY! to you, evildoer!

Eugene thought. *Your evil itchy plan of cootie itchiness will never ever succeed on this day, Little Miss Stinky Pinky! Captain Awesome and Nacho Cheese Man will fight your cooties before they itch again!*

Eugene quickly scratched his left arm.

CHAPTER 4

Peas of
Doom and Destruction
and YUCK

By Eugene

"Now this is our lunch line," Ms. Beasley said to Sally as she proudly pointed out how students get their trays and their forks and wait in line for their food.

Well, DUH.

Eugene wanted to ask Sally to sit with him and Charlie. He remembered his first day at school and how nice it was that Charlie had sat with him.

As a Super Dude fan, Eugene tried to follow Super Dude's "Motto of Niceness" from Super Dude No. 1, No. 15, No. 29, and No. 158: "Being nice is super, so be supernice, dude!"

Before Eugene could say anything to Sally, he smelled a yucky stink! Not the diaper yuck of his nemesis Queen Stinkypants from Planet Baby, but the stinky yuck of another bad guy, the evil cafeteria cook known as **Dr. Spinach!**

Dr. Spinach was a villain so YUCKY, even his first name was

YUCK! Dr. Yuck Spinach.

"Be alert, Nacho Cheese Man," Eugene whispered. "Dr. Spinach is back, and this time, he's brought his most evil round sidekicks . . ."

Charlie gasped. "Noooo! Not. The. Green. Peas!"

"Yes, PEAS!"

"AAAAAAAAAAAAAAAAAAAA
AAAAAAA!" the two boys shouted
in unison. You'd think the other kids
in the cafeteria would've turned
to look, but everyone was pretty
much used to Eugene and Charlie
shouting AAAAAAAAAAAAAAAA
AAAAAAAAA! in the lunch line.

"YUCK! The only vegetable
worse than bok choy,"
Eugene groaned.

Test tubes filled with gravy
bubbled behind Dr. Spinach.
Pots and pans foamed over

with saucy, red Pasta Potions.

"Welcome to the cafeteria, boys!" Dr. Spinach cackled and evilly twirled the ends of his curly, evil mustache.

That's a whole lotta evil, Eugene thought.

With his greasy hairnet and his cackling chicken-laugh, Dr. Spinach was determined to serve Eugene and Charlie his yucky, green, round food of doom!

He knows yucky green peas can steal my Captain Awesome superpowers! thought Eugene.

Professor Beano Greenstalk, in Super Dude No. 19, tried to turn Super Dude into plant food with his slimy Asparagus Ray. But his friends, the Rabbit Rangers from Carrotopia, hopped into battle and kicked Professor Beano Greenstalk right in the cabbage patch. "Never doubt the power of long ears and soft fur," Super Dude said as he tossed Professor Beano Greenstalk onto the compost heap.

Eugene and Charlie had no choice. They'd have to fight their way past Dr. Spinach's Lunch Line of Greasy Terror before he could blast them with school board-approved peas.

"Whatever you do, don't look at him!" Eugene warned. "His Evil Spinach Eyes will zap you!"

CHAPTER 5

The Creature from the Litter Box

LITTER BOX

By Eugene

"Jane has five apples. Jimmy has two more apples than Jane. Karen has one less apple than Jimmy. How many apples does Karen have?"

Where did these kids get all these apples? Eugene wondered. *And why in the world would any kid need six apples?*

But still, homework had to be done. And Eugene was doing it. Until he heard the noise outside his window.

meow.

What was that?

"MEOW." Again.

A cat! At the window! Eugene was instantly suspicious. Was it the Meow Mixer, ready to cough up a Hyper Furball at him?! Or the very bad Katty McKlaw with plans to scratch?! Or *something* WORSE!?

Eugene crept to the window. He threw open the curtains!

"Time to clean your litter box, Katty McKlaw!"

Oh. It was just an ordinary cat on the windowsill. Turbo's wheel stopped spinning. Turbo gave the cat a cold stare.

A funny-looking orange cat that looked a lot like orange juice if orange juice had four legs, with little white stripes and green eyes.

"Ew. Peas." The sight of green made Eugene think of the hated vegetable.

Eugene decided right away to call it Funny Cat.

Funny Cat jumped through the open window. Turbo raced to the far edge of his cage and turned his back to the cat with a snort.

Eugene had always wanted a cat . . . and Captain Awesome could use another reliable sidekick, especially one that could use its Claws of

Goodness to catch an evil mouse or climb an evil tree. Eugene rubbed Funny Cat's head.

"Purr," the cat purred.

"Aw, Mom and Dad would never go for another pet." Eugene sighed. As he carried Funny Cat back to the window, a thought popped into his head.

They don't have to know about Funny Cat yet, right?

"I'll bet you have all kinds of awesome cat powers!" Eugene said.

Turbo began running as fast as he could on his wheel.

"Meow," the cat lazily meowed and licked its paw.

"I knew it! You've probably got nine lives and you can always land on your feet!" The possibilities excited Eugene. "Oh! What if Captain Awesome had a cat sidekick . . . oh man! That would totally growl up Mr. Drools!"

Turbo stopped spinning on his wheel and looked right at Eugene.

ZIP! **FOLD!** **FLUFF!**

In a flash Eugene made a comfy bed for Funny Cat in his closet then jumped into his own bed. He pulled the covers up to his head, safe and snug with the thought of having a new, furry friend in the battle against the bad guys.

And then came that howl he would know anywhere! Mr. Drools was back!

HOWWWWWWWWWWWWL!

Eugene bolted upright in his bed. "Looks like that dangerous dog is up past his bedtime!" Eugene said to Funny Cat and Turbo.

YES!

"Come on, Turbo! Let's introduce Mr. Drools to the newest member of the Sunnyview Superhero Squad! Time to give that tail-wagging do-badder a meowful!"

***S**queak. Squeak. Squeak.*

Dr. Yuck Spinach pushed a squeaky cart piled high with boxes of frozen peas down the hall of Sunnyview Elementary.

"Peas, peas, good for your heart! Peas, peas, you'll get a good start! Peas for lunch and peas for dinner! Eat your peas and be a winner!" he sang.

Pure evil!

After Dr. Spinach disappeared into the cafeteria, Eugene and Charlie stepped out from their hiding place behind the bathroom door.

The boys scurried down the hall and outside. Not even evil could make them miss recess.

Sally sat by herself on the steps and quietly

stared at her shoes. Again.

"Hey, what's wrong, Sally?" Eugene said.

Sally burst into tears. "I never wanted to move to Sunnyview! I hate this place! I wanted to stay with my friends! And worst of all," Sally said, "Mr. Whiskersworth has run away."

"Mr. Whiskersworth?" Charlie asked. "Is that your dad?"

"No, my cat."

"What does your cat look like?" Eugene asked.

Sally pulled out a picture of

Mr. Whiskersworth. He was orange, like the color of orange juice if orange juice had four legs, with little white stripes and green eyes.

"Ew. Peas." The sight of green made Eugene think of the hated vegetable.

Mr. Whiskersworth looks just like Funny Cat, Eugene thought. *Maybe they're brothers!*

But before Eugene could say

anything, Sally burst into tears again and ran back into the class-room.

"She's so upset she's going to miss recess?" Eugene said, surprised.

"Wow. I didn't think it was possible to be that upset," Charlie replied.

"This sounds like a job for the Sunnyview Superhero Squad," Eugene said.

The boys were about to leap into action to find the guilty Whiskersworth-napper when a voice called out from the swings behind them.

"We're going to beat you today, Eugene!" It was Mike Flinch.

Bernie Melnik was at his side and stabbed a finger toward the two boys. "Yeah!" Bernie wasn't much of a talker.

Bernie and Mike were both epic

swing jumpers—they could launch themselves off a swing like two elementary school bananas in a slingshot—but could they beat Captain Awesome and Nacho Cheese Man?

"Let Flinch and Melnik beware!" Eugene said.

Intergalactic swing-jumping is one of my many playground super-powers.

Bravely, Captain Awesome and Nacho Cheese Man grabbed their swings and prepared to jump through the rings of Saturn. . . .

CHAPTER 7

Nacho Cheese Man Has a Secret Power You Wish You Had

By Eugene

Was there anything greater than going home from school after such a great victory? Nope. Eugene and Charlie laughed and high-fived all the way home.

Eugene interrupted the happiness with a serious thought. "A cat  that looks *exactly* like Sally's photo of Mr. Whiskersworth came to my room last night. . . ."

"I'll bet it's Mr. Whiskersworth's brother!" Charlie exclaimed.

"I was thinking the *saaaaame* thing," Eugene said. "If only one of us could speak Cat, then we could ask Funny Cat if he knows where Mr. Whiskersworth is!"

"Then it's a good thing one of us *does* speak Cat," Charlie said, then added a meow.

"No. Way."

"Oh yes. Way. I have more than just the power of canned cheese," Charlie said. "I have power over the animals. I can get a dog to come to

me when I call its name. I can pet a dolphin. And I can get a seagull to catch a french fry in midair. Guaranteed!"

Eugene was impressed. *There's a lot more to Nacho Cheese Man than I thought. We'll have to start making a list of our powers!*

"Did you ever wonder how I first discovered Mr. Drools's rotten, no-good plans?"

"Wow! You can read Dog, too?!" Eugene gasped.

"No! Are you nuts?! Everyone knows dogs can't write! But I

can read their doggie minds. Now take me to this cat!" Charlie commanded in his most heroic and commanding voice ever. "But first I gotta ask my mom if I can go over to your house, okay? I think I have piano lessons."

CHAPTER 8

Shh . . . It's the Cat Whisperer

By
Eugene

Hiss!

Captain Awesome stuck out his hand to pet Funny Cat. "It's okay."

SCRATCH!

"Are you sure he's one of the good guys?" Nacho Cheese Man asked.

Captain Awesome was wondering the same thing. And then he realized the problem!

319

"Nacho Cheese Man is one of the good guys, Funny Cat! And don't worry, he didn't put a mind-control cheese helmet on my head to make me say that."

"I know what'll convince him." Nacho Cheese Man squirted a bit of cheese onto his finger and held it under the cat's nose. Funny Cat licked the cheese.

"He likes it!" Captain Awesome said.

"Duh. It's cheese." Clearing his throat, Nacho Cheese Man looked into Funny Cat's eyes.

"OMMMMMM!"

he chanted, startling Captain Awesome. "What? It helps me get our brains in tune. OMMMMM!" he chanted again, then leaned closer to Funny Cat. "Funny Cat, where is your brother, Mr. Whiskersworth?" Nacho Cheese Man asked in a commanding voice. He watched Funny Cat lick. "Very interesting . . ."

"What'd he say?" an eager Captain Awesome asked.

"He says he's a cat. And that he loves cheese."

"What about Mr. Whiskersworth?" Captain Awesome asked.

"Oh yeah. I almost forgot." Nacho Cheese Man locked eyes with Funny Cat and in a serious voice

asked, "Do you know where your brother, Mr. Whiskersworth, is?"

There was a short pause as Funny Cat cleaned his whiskers.

"Yes, yes," Nacho Cheese Man said, a bit impatient. "I got that part already. You love cheese. But where is Mr.—"

RUFFFF!

"It's Mr. Drools again!" Captain Awesome yelled. "He's come back for my Frisbee!"

Funny Cat jumped through the open window. He scurried across the roof and climbed down the big maple tree near Eugene's house.

"Wow! Look at Funny Cat go!" Nacho Cheese Man cheered. "The Sunnyview Superhero Squad is right behind you!"

Captain Awesome grabbed Turbo and tucked him into his Turbomobile. "Time to get **MI-TEE!**"

Earth's two greatest heroes not named Super Dude jumped into the teleporter bay and beamed up to the Dog Star to battle the menace of Mr. Drools once more.

Neither hero spoke. This was serious super-hero business. After all, the fate of the world's greatest Frisbee was hanging in the balance.

CHAPTER 9

So the New Neighbor Isn't an Alien Spy After All

By Eugene

"**E**pic!" Captain Awesome said. His Frisbee was safe again. Mr. Drools had been defeated by the Sunnyview Superhero Squad. "Let doggie-do-badders take note: Not rain nor snow nor too much homework will keep the Sunnyview Superhero Squad from upholding all that is good, right, and . . ."

"Covered in chocolate!" added Nacho Cheese Man.

"Well, I was going to say 'true,' but 'covered in chocolate' isn't bad, either," Captain Awesome admitted.

Captain Awesome picked up Funny Cat. "Ready for a little more mind reading?"

But before Nacho Cheese Man could read any more minds, Funny Cat jumped from Captain Awesome's hands and raced away.

Whoa! I can't lose a cat I just found! thought Eugene.

Both Captain Awesome and Nacho Cheese Man took off after Funny Cat. They ran down the sidewalk, through Mr. Muckelberry's front yard—he hates when kids do that—jumped over the bushes, and fell into Mrs. Humbert's begonias—she hates when kids do that.

Funny Cat was faster than the lightning from the fingertips of Captain Lightning Fingertips from Super Dude No. 68. He teamed up with King Thunder Toes to rain on Super Dude's Super Dude Parade. Luckily, it was only cloudy with a slight chance of defeat for the bad guys and it was the Super Dudiest parade ever.

Captain Awesome and Nacho Cheese Man screeched to a stop at

the end of the cul-de-sac.

"Uh, Eugene, do you know where we are?"

Funny Cat had led them to the house where the alien spies had just moved in. "We have to get

Funny Cat back before the alien spies hook him up to their alien spy machines and suck out his super-smart cat brain."

"We need a Plan A!" said Nacho Cheese Man.

"And Plans B and C, just in case!"

CRASH!

"What was that?!" said Captain Awesome and Nacho Cheese Man

at the exact same time.

There was no time for any plans, A, B, and certainly not C! It was time for action!

Together Captain Awesome and Nacho Cheese Man ran to the side of the alien spy house where they found four things that each required their own exclamation marks:

1. Sally Williams!

2. Her bike!

3. Trash cans!

4. Funny Cat (sitting on top of the pile, purring and licking his paw like nothing had happened)!

"Are you okay?!" asked Captain Awesome as he helped Sally from the pile of trash cans.

"Mr. Whiskersworth!" Sally was too excited to care about crashing her bike into the trash cans. "You found him!" She looked at the boys in their superhero outfits. "Whoever you're supposed to be."

"I am Captain Awesome!" said Captain Awesome in his most heroic voice ever.

"And I am Nacho Cheese Man," Nacho Cheese Man said, in his most heroic voice ever. He added a heroic pose because you can never be too heroic at times like this.

"We're the Sunnyview Superhero Squad," Captain Awesome explained. "And you're in big danger! This is an alien spy house!"

"Don't be silly," Sally laughed. "This is my house. We just moved in." She gave Mr. Whiskersworth a big, happy squeeze.

Captain Awesome recognized Sally's bike from the moving van. He leaped into action and checked Sally's hair.

"What are you doing?!" Sally said and pulled away.

"Looking for an alien mind-control helmet," Captain Awesome explained, then turned to Nacho Cheese Man. "She's all clear. No alien spyness here."

"Wait a second." A realization hit Nacho Cheese Man. "You called Funny Cat 'Mr. Whiskersworth . . .'"

"Well, *yeah*," Sally hugged the

cat again. "This *is* my cat. See?" Sally showed the boys the cat's collar. It read Mr. Whiskersworth.

SHOCK!

"*THAT'S* Mr. Whiskersworth?!" Captain Awesome gasped. He scrunched his nose and looked at Nacho Cheese Man.

"What? I would've figured that out if the cat didn't keep thinking about how much he loved cheese," Nacho Cheese Man said, defending himself.

"He's right! Mr. Whiskersworth does love cheese!" Sally offered.

"See! I knew it! I was right!" Nacho Cheese Man proudly puffed out his chest, then continued, "I bet Mr. Whiskersworth ran away because he was sad that you and your family had to move."

"I was sad to leave too,"

Sally said. "But I'm glad that Mr. Whiskersworth is back."

Captain Awesome was silent. As Sally and Nacho Cheese Man talked, he had a tough decision

to make—even tougher than the time his mom had asked him if he wanted green beans or eggplant with dinner.

Funny Cat belonged to Sally. The duty of any and all super-heroes was to return lost cats to their owners. Even if you really, really, really, like *really*, wanted to keep them for yourself.

Eugene remembered the time that Meredith Mooney hamster-napped poor Turbo. He didn't want to make anyone feel as bad as he had felt on that day.

"Could I have a moment alone with Mr. Whiskersworth?" Captain Awesome asked. Sally handed over her cat and the world's greatest hero who was not named Super Dude gave him a final hug. "I hope you enjoyed being my second sidekick as much as I enjoyed having you as a second sidekick," the

heroic boy whispered into the cat's ear. "Be brave, be good."

"Meow," the cat replied, and Captain Awesome knew that everything would be all right.

"Thanks, Captain Awesome and Nacho Cheese Man, for finding Mr. Whiskersworth. He's my best friend, and I'm so glad he's home." Sally put Mr. Whiskersworth in the basket on her bike. "Now we're going to patrol—I mean *explore* the neighborhood."

"Just be sure to remember to stay out of Mr. Muckelberry's yard,"

Nacho Cheese Man suggested. "He's kinda upset right now." Down the street, Mr. Muckelberry was standing in his front yard, shaking his fist at them.

"We'll go apologize after he's calmed down a little." In his normal Eugene voice, Captain Awesome said to Sally, "I'm glad you got your cat back, Sally. Maybe you'll like Sunnyview more now."

"I think I will."

Sally rode her bicycle down the driveway and into the street. Captain Awesome and Nacho

Cheese Man watched to make sure
she used all the proper
turn signals. And
she did.

"What a
great day!"
Captain
Awesome
said.

"Villains bravely defeated, a second sidekick . . . for a while . . . a chase through Sunnyview, and maybe even a new friend to—"

WAIT A MINUTE!

And that was the moment when Captain Awesome saw **IT**.

SUPER DUDE!

It was one of the most amazing ITs he had ever, ever seen in, like, forever.

"Check out her bicycle!"

Nacho Cheese Man saw it too! On the back of her seat was a Super Dude license plate.

A Super Dude license plate!

SALLY WAS A SUPER DUDE FAN TOO!

"We've really got to get one of those!" Nacho Cheese Man said.

Captain Awesome agreed.

But Captain Awesome couldn't fight the feeling that there was more to Sally than he had originally thought. Could it be that Sally Williams was much more than a mild-mannered girl, new kid on the block, and cat lover? Could it be that she had a power more awesome than just being able to stare at her shoes all day long?

Could it be . . . wondered Captain Awesome. *Could it be that Sally is secretly a superhero, too?*

Sally disappeared around the corner on her bike and Captain Awesome knew his question would just have to wait . . . for now.

THE

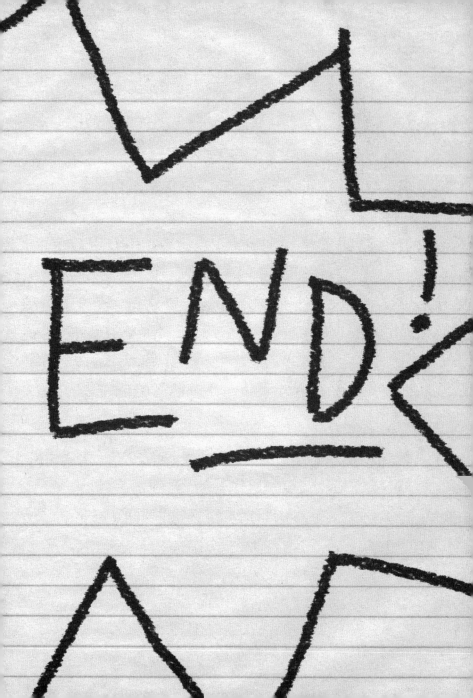

CAPTAIN AWESOME

VS. THE
SPOOKY, SCARY HOUSE

Table of Contents

CHAPTER I

Halloween, Halloween

By Eugene

"Boo!"

Eugene McGillicudy pedaled his bike next to his best friend, Charlie Thomas Jones.

Could Halloween be any more awesome? Eugene thought.

There were the jack-o'-lanterns, the falling leaves, the chill of the autumn air. And best of all . . .

TRICK OR TREAT!

There was the dressing up in

costumes and running from house to house to collect as much candy and chocolate as your hands—or backs—could carry!

You didn't get that amount of awesomeness on Presidents' Day or even on a snow day.

And Halloween was getting closer.

Eugene and Charlie took the long way home from school. They pedaled slowly, their eyes darting from side to side. The dry fall leaves swirled across the street and crunched under the wheels of their bikes.

The town of Sunnyview went all out for Halloween. Houses were

covered in fake spider-webs and pumpkins were on every porch. One yard had a mummy in a coffin, and another had Frankenstein sitting in a rocking chair. But Eugene and Charlie weren't just enjoying the spooky scenes.

They were out on patrol.

MONSTER PATROL!

For real monsters, Halloween was like their birthday. It was a chance for them to run freely around Sunnyview without anyone thinking twice about it. In the dark no one could tell the difference between the real Count Fangula and Kieran Phillips in a vampire costume.

"You see any evil yet, Charlie?" Eugene asked.

"Just a torn paper skeleton," Charlie responded.

The boys were determined to stop Halloween evil. No monsters would ruin the greatest day in the history of free candy! Eugene and Charlie would stop them because that's what their favorite superhero, Super Dude, would do.

What's that you say?

You've never heard of Super Dude? WHAT?! Do you not have all of his comic books, movies, video games, and action figures?

Super Dude is the super superhero who once washed the evil Liquid Fury down the drain in *Super Dude and the Clean Car Wash of Cleanliness.*

Super Dude was a true hero and Eugene's favorite. He was, after all, the main reason Eugene became Sunnyview's first and most awesome superhero. Eugene was the one, the only . . . CAPTAIN AWESOME!

MI-TEE!

With his best friend, Charlie Thomas Jones (also known as the

superhero Nacho Cheese Man), and their class pet hamster, Turbo, Eugene formed the Sunnyview Superhero Squad to stop the eviling of bad guys.

SKID!

Eugene skidded
to a stop at the edge
of Mr. Muckleberry's
driveway. A tingle ran
up his arm and zipped through
his whole body.

"What is it, Eugene?" Charlie
asked. He could tell Eugene was
sensing something bad.

"Shhh. Over there." Eugene
pointed across the lawn. . . .

CHAPTER 2

The Scarecroaker!

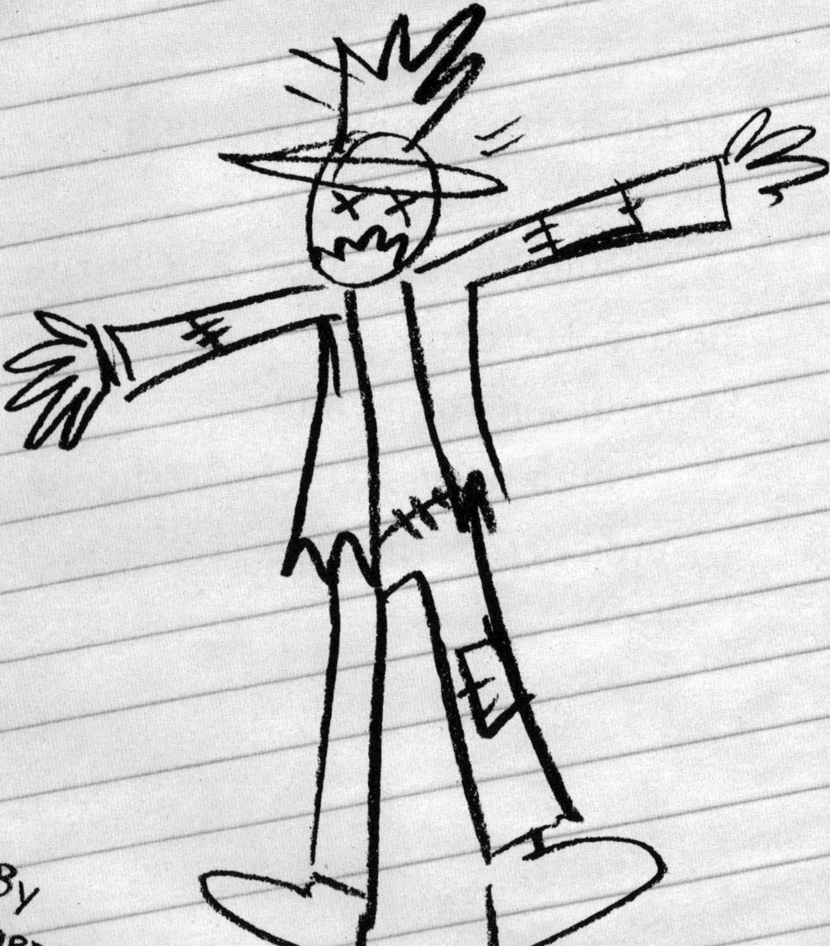

By
Eugene

A creature stood next to Mr. Muckleberry. But not just any creature. It was the enemy of pumpkins and children everywhere: **the Scarecroaker!**

The awful scarecrow had a straw-stuffed body, floppy hat, and burlap mask covering his face. Looking like a normal scarecrow was just one of his many powers.

But Eugene knew better. The

Scarecroaker was trouble. He was just a few straws away from Mr. Muckleberry, who was working quietly in his yard hanging tiny plastic pumpkins from his maple tree.

"Mr. Muckleberry! Look out!" the boys shouted in unison.

Mr. Muckleberry didn't speak.

Oh no! He's been hypnotized by the Scarecroaker's Straw Trance! Eugene thought.

This was just like that time in the Super Dude Creepy Halloween Special No. 2, when Super Dude battled the Vampirates and their fleet of Flying Coffin Ships. He turned their wooden ships into splinters, which had, in turn, turned the Vampirates into dust.

Stopping the Scarecroaker was a job for the Sunnyview Superhero Squad!

"Hey, Scarecroaker! Stay away from Mr. Muckleberry, you evil scarecrow made of straw!" Captain Awesome jumped the MI-TEE Mobile over the curb and pedaled across Mr. Muckleberry's lawn.

"We are going to knock your stuffing into November!" Captain Awesome yelled to the Scarecroaker.

"What he said!" Nacho Cheese Man added. He pulled a can of cheese from his backpack and steered the Cheesy Rider up the driveway. "Cheesy YO!"

CHAPTER 3

Do You Know Where We Are?

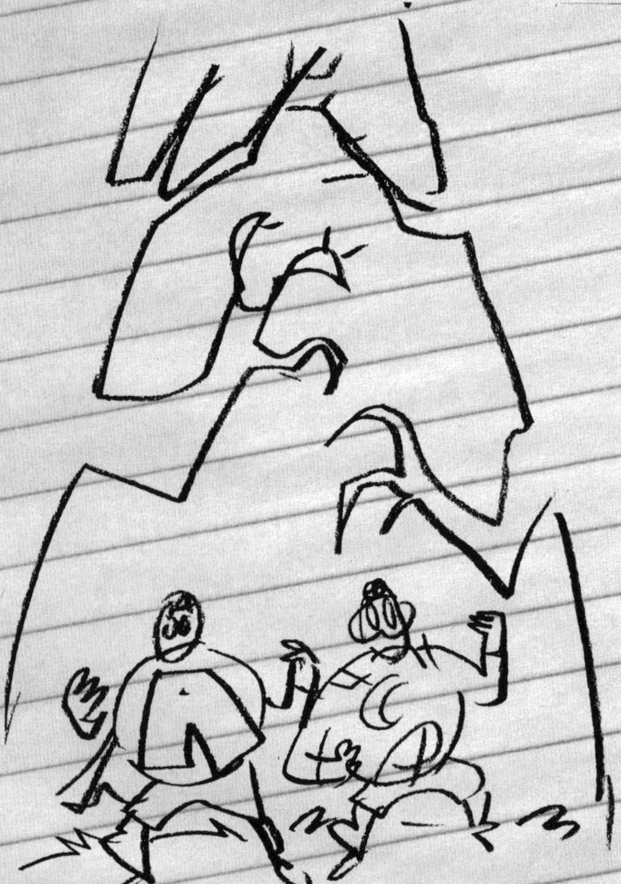

By Eugene

Hmmmmm. Eugene was thinking.

Hmmmmm. Eugene was thinking harder.

Hmmmmm! Ouch! He was thinking so hard his head hurt.

"Eugene?" Charlie said. "Where *are* we?"

After defeating the very evil Scarecroaker, the superheroes had sped away superfast from

Mr. Muckleberry's house. He hadn't had time to thank Captain Awesome and Nacho Cheese Man for saving his life since he was too busy raking up all the scattered straw from his lawn.

The superheroes zigged, then zagged, doubled back, turned right four times, left four times, and cut through Mr. Worth's pumpkin patch, down a dirt road, through a gravel alley, and then stopped to catch their breath.

SKID!

They ended up on the street where their friend Sally Williams lived. Her house had a glowing jack-o'-lantern on the porch and

ghosts hanging in all the windows.

"We should go say hi to Sally," Charlie suggested.

"Not now, Charlie. Look!" At the end of the street was something Eugene had never noticed before. Eugene was pointing to a yard overgrown with trees that looked like they were eating the ground under them.

FLASH!

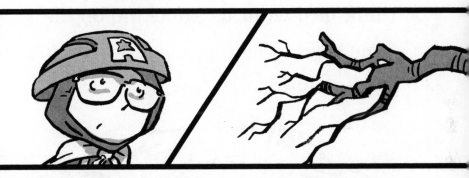

Gasp! What was that? Eugene thought. *Is there something in the trees?*

"Charlie! My Super-Awesome Super-Vision is detecting something worth seeing. Let's go check it out."

A chill went up Charlie's spine. "Eugene! Wait! What if that's the house where the deadly Manguar, half man, half jaguar, lives? I don't think he'd want us knocking on his front door."

Too late.

Eugene jumped his bike up onto the curb and headed through the trees. Charlie sighed and pedaled to catch up.

Eugene powered through the trees that were trying to grab him and the branches that were trying to scratch him.

Charlie blasted through the jungle behind him. "Eugene! Where are you?" Charlie pushed the branches out of his way, struggling to keep his balance. "Eugene!"

Suddenly Charlie stumbled across Eugene's bike. But where

was Eugene? Charlie got off his bike and ran out of the trees. Eugene was waiting for him. A large, three-story house was in front of them.

"Look at this place, Charlie."

Sunlight gleamed off a broken attic window. The front door flopped open as if someone had punched it, shutters on the upstairs windows were crooked, and the porch railing was missing pieces. Paint was peeling so much that it looked like the house had a bad sunburn.

No one had lived there for a long time.

383

Eugene and Charlie dropped to the ground. They crept along the grass toward the front porch.

Eugene peeked over the edge. The porch was empty. "Come on, Charlie."

Charlie gulped as he followed Eugene. Keeping low to the ground, they reached the stairs.

"I think my Awesome Sense is tingling again," Eugene said.

"I think it's your Creepy Sense," Charlie said. "This house is creepy. Those windows look like eyes."

Charlie was right. Worse, the door looked like a crooked mouth laughing at them. The roof and the chimney looked like an evil top hat.

Eugene realized the horrible truth. "Charlie! This is no ordinary house at the end of an ordinary street. This house is here on purpose."

"On purpose? For people to live in, right?" Charlie asked.

"Wrong, my superhero friend! This is a house of no good!"

"I was afraid you'd say that," Charlie replied, shaking his head.

Eugene took one step forward, then paused. His whole body was tingling. He felt weird. His hands were sweaty. He looked over to where he'd left his bike. "It's getting

late. We should come back later."

Charlie started backing up across the yard.

The sun was setting. Long shadows fell across the front of the house. "You're right, Eugene. Besides, I have to get home for, uh, dinner," Charlie said. "And other kinds of stuff."

Eugene was quick to agree. "I've got to finish tonight's homework. Maybe tomorrow night's, too."

Charlie nodded. "Yep, nothing wrong with doing homework."

Eugene and Charlie ran over to their bikes and pushed them through the trees. Back on the street they hopped on the bikes and headed for home.

They made it in record time.

CHAPTER 4

The Creepy House Is Really . . . Creepy

By
Eugene

"Hello, house. We meet again."

That night, Eugene climbed the stairs to the porch of the abandoned house. Shadows from the overgrown trees made everything darker. And creepier.

SCRATCH!

Tree branches scraped across the windows. Eugene swallowed a lump that felt like a golf ball. He

pushed open the front door and
stepped inside the house.

CREEEEEEEEEAAKKK!

He was alone. At night. Inside the creepy old house.

Why am I here by myself? Eugene wondered.

The house was as dark as the inside of Captain Darkness's all-powerful Midnight Helmet. A breeze chilled the air and Eugene shivered.

BRRRRR.

Eugene's hand felt along the wall, trying to find a light switch. *Got it!*

CLICK!

Nothing.

CLICK-CLICK-CLICK-CLICK!

Still nothing.

Eugene smacked the wall with his hand.

WHAP!

Still no lights.

Good thing there's a full moon, Eugene thought. The moonlight shone in through the dusty, broken windows, cutting long rectangles across the wooden floor.

Eugene suddenly felt nervous. He reminded himself that superheroes may get scared, but they're still superheroes. He'd learned that from Super Dude No. 14, when Super Dude was afraid to enter Mr. Bones's Zombie Cemetery.

Super Dude went in anyway. If Super Dude could do something like that, then Eugene knew he could too. He placed his right foot onto the first step of the staircase in front of him.

CREAK!

That was the problem with old
stairs. They always creaked.

Eugene went for the
second step.

MEOW!

A black cat
jumped off the
stairs. By the time
Eugene turned to look,
the cat was gone.

Eugene shivered and climbed
the second step . . . then the third.

CREAK-CREAK!

And then he heard something
else entirely.

What was that thump? Eugene froze on the stairs like he'd been hit with a blast of Frozen Freak's Freeze Gas.

THUMP-THUMP-THUMP!

Footsteps!

THUMP-THUMP-THUMP!

The footsteps were on the second

floor. Running. And they were getting closer. Someone or some*thing*
was coming toward him.

Eugene turned to run down the
stairs. The footsteps were coming
after him. Eugene's legs felt like
rubber. His feet were like concrete
blocks. He had to get away.

Eugene fell down the stairs and crashed onto the floor.

OOF!

He held his breath and listened. Closer . . . closer . . . The footsteps were at the top of the stairs now. Eugene turned and saw a shadow looking down at him. He wanted to scream, but his mouth was locked tight.

"Eep" was all that came out. Eugene scrambled to his feet and ran toward the front door.

SLAM! He crashed into the door and dropped to the floor.

401

That was when Eugene woke up in his bed.

He sat up. He was shaking and sweaty. He looked around his bedroom. His Super Dude poster was on the wall. Turbo was still in his hamster cage. He was home. *A DREAM! It was all just a dream!*

No, not a dream. A nightmare!
WHEW!

"Turbo! You wouldn't believe the nightmare I had," Eugene said to the hamster.

SQUEAK-SQUEAK-SQUEAK!

Turbo was happily spinning on his wheel, unaware of the horror Eugene had just gone through.

Eugene wondered why he was nightmaring about that creepy old house. Was the house sending him a message? Or was there a new villain in Sunnyview, like the Dream Beaver or Nightmare Gnat, who was invading his sleep?

I've got to tell Charlie about this in the morning, thought Eugene.

And morning couldn't come soon enough.

CHAPTER 5

Welcome to My Nightmare

By
Eugene

"I'll be a zombie!" Bernie Melnick said. "Braaaiiiinnnnssss!"

"I'm going to be a princess!" Jessica Craven exclaimed.

"I'm going to be a *zombie* princess," said Mike Flinch. "I mean, prince. Zombie prince."

School was buzzing the next day. Halloween was getting closer, and everyone was excited about their costumes.

Evan Mason even had the perfect Halloween equation. "If I wear a pirate costume with two swords, plus two eye patches, and say 'yo ho ho trick or treat,' I'll get twice as much candy as anyone else. It's a scientific fact!"

But Eugene had something else on his mind: his nightmare. He'd been trying to tell Charlie about

it all morning, but school kept getting in the way. . . .

"Hey, Charlie!"

BRRRINNGGG! The school bell
rang.

"Hey, Charlie!"

"Please, Eugene, no talking in
class," his teacher Ms. Beasley said.

"Hey, Charlie!"

"Shhhhhh! Quiet in my library," the school librarian shushed him. Eugene recognized her right away as the twisted bookshelf mastermind, The Shusher!

By lunchtime Eugene was about to burst. He raced over to the table where Charlie was squirting blasts of Barbecue Cheese spray on the cafeteria's Surprise Nuggets.

"I've got to tell you about my nightmare. I was at the house," Eugene said. "*THE* house."

"The house that gives out the full-size candy bars and lets us go back for seconds?" Charlie asked.

"No," Eugene corrected. "The

creepy house on Sally's street!"

Charlie's mouth fell open. His eyes got wide.

Eugene continued. "I was there in my dream, I mean, my nightmare! There were footsteps and a creaky staircase! Then— *THUMP!*—some-one or something came after me."

"Wow, Eugene! That's fantastic!" Charlie took a

deep breath and sucked down the last spray of canned cheese. He smiled. "I don't know how else to say it," he said. "It sounds like you got a new superpower! You can see into the future!"

"But I—"

"No buts," Charlie said. "We're going to win every game of dodgeball! Even better: You'll know exactly when my mom's going to serve okra so I can ask to eat dinner at *your* house."

"But I don't—"

"Knowing the future is the perfect superpower!" Charlie was so excited that he was practically floating on thin air.

"Charlie, I can't see into the

future!" Eugene yelled. "I think it was just a nightmare."

Charlie slumped onto his chair. "That's too bad. Nightmares won't help me avoid okra at all."

"But there *is* something about that old house, Charlie. Something scary," Eugene said. "And we're going to find out what that is."

"We're going to find out by looking on the Internet, right, Eugene?"

Eugene's chuckle sent a chill up Charlie's spine. He knew what Eugene was thinking.

"This is a job for the Sunnyview Superhero Squad," Eugene said. "Captain Awesome and Nacho Cheese Man have to protect the citizens of Sunnyview from that creepy old house and whatever evil may be lurking inside it!"

Charlie sighed. "A superhero

has to do what a superhero has to do," he said, nodding. That was Super Dude's motto. "I'll get an extra supply of canned cheese."

CHAPTER 6

The Double Dog Dare

BY
Eugene

"Soggy French fries are the best!" Jake Story cried. He grabbed a cold, limp French fry from the cafeteria food line and popped it into his mouth. He smiled and pushed the mushy mess through his front teeth with his tongue.

Usually Charlie and Eugene were more than eager to join Jake in grossing out the girls with a mushy food frenzy, but today was

different. Today was *serious*.

"We've gotta figure out how to get into that house, Charlie," Eugene said. "Any ideas?"

"Maybe we can ask our dads to go with us?" Charlie asked hopefully. "You know, as sort of a 'take your dad to superhero duty day'?"

"No way, dude!" said Eugene.

"We're trained superheroes! Our dads may be experts at barbecuing, but we don't know what's inside that house! It might have tentacles or fifty eyeballs or fifty tentacles with eyeballs!"

"F-fifty eyeballs?" Charlie looked at his cheese-covered lunch. He suddenly wasn't very hungry anymore.

"I know exactly what's in that house," Meredith Mooney said as she sat down at the last open spot at Eugene and

Charlie's table. Both boys slid away from Meredith to make room for her pigtails tied with pink ribbons. Her ribbons matched her pink shoes, pink socks, and pink dress.

"Hey! They were saving that place for me!" Sally Williams said, holding her tray of food.

Meredith stuck out her tongue and turned back to Charlie and Eugene. Sally sighed and sat at the next table.

Meredith turned back to the boys. "My older sister, Mary, went inside that house last Halloween on a double dog dare," she told them.

GASP!

Meredith's claim was met with gasps from kids at several tables.

"Double dog?" Eugene let out a soft whistle.

"Now, that's one serious dare," Charlie said, shaking his head.

"Well, you don't just go into a house like that on a *normal* dare, do you?" Meredith said with a snarl. "The moon was full . . . and it was a dark, dark night! My sister opened the door and went inside, but none of the lights worked."

Just like my dream! Eugene thought.

"And then she heard it! *CREAK! STOMP-STOMP! CREAK! STOMP! MOAN! GROAN!*" Meredith said.

Eugene's eyes were bigger than baseballs. He sat in stunned silence. *I don't believe it! I dreamed that, too!*

Meredith continued. "My sister turned and looked . . . and she saw the headless ghost of the Sunny-view Spirit!"

"Ah! I hate ghosts!" Jake Story shouted, and ran away from the

cafeteria, leaving behind a full
plate of cold fries.

No one else moved a muscle.
They all stared at Meredith Mooney
like they were zombies.

"The S-S-Sunnyview S-Spirit?!"
Charlie stammered.

"The one and only," Meredith
said spookily.

"What's the Sunnyview Spirit?"
Eugene asked.

"Oh, please!" Meredith snapped.
"Haven't you been listening? He's

a headless ghost who lives in the house! He came floating down the stairs, holding his head in his hands. Because that's what headless ghosts do. *'Grooooan!'* he groaned. *'Moaaaaaan!'* he moaned. *'Booooo!'* he booed! And then he tried to grab my sister!"

"Did she get away?" asked Sally, who was listening from the next table.

"Of course she did." Meredith rolled her eyes. "No ghost without a head is a match for *my* big sister. But the Sunnyview Spirit warned her that the next nosy kid who comes snooping around *his* house won't be so lucky. I'm sure you two are too chicken to go back there anyway."

The kids in the cafeteria looked at Charlie and Eugene, waiting for their response. Even Sally watched.

"Just because we're afraid doesn't mean we're chicken—" Eugene began.

"Yeah!" Charlie added.

"And nothing you say will make us feel bad if we *don't* go to that house—" Eugene continued.

"Yeah! Nothing you can say!" Charlie added.

"But we're still gonna go and check out this ghost story," Eugene finished.

"Yeah! We're still gonna go!" Charlie's eyes went wide. He pulled

Eugene aside. "What do you mean we're still gonna go?! Didn't you hear Meredith's story with the ghost and the head and GROAAAAAAN?"

"Did Super Dude back down when he went up against the Zombie Teachers in the School of Screams? They wanted him to do impossible math problems *and* eat brains. Even a superhero gets scared, Charlie.

But that should never stop us from doing what's good and right. And if this ghost is a bad guy, we've got to protect Sunnyview."

Charlie slumped. "I hate it when you make sense."

It looked like Halloween night was going to be *extra* spooky this year.

CHAPTER 7

Beware of the Sneaky Sneakers!

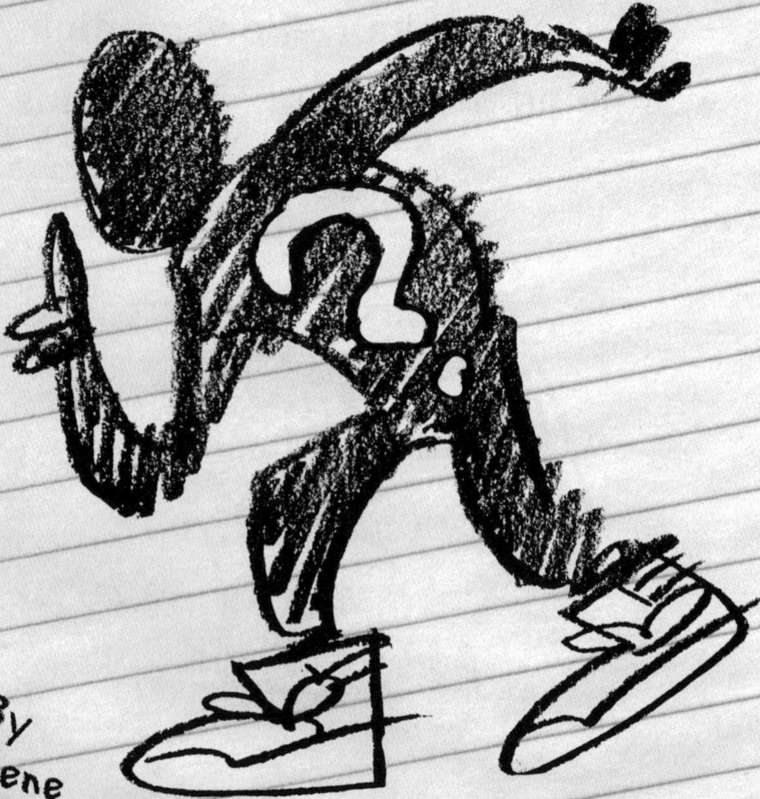

By Eugene

Captain Awesome and Nacho Cheese Man called an emergency meeting of the Sunnyview Superhero Squad. They sat under the school-yard slide. Today they had much more to worry about than the cafeteria's mushy food. Meredith's story about the Sunnyview Spirit made them realize they were about to face their spookiest villain yet!

"But why do we have to go on

Halloween night?" Nacho Cheese Man asked as he very nervously squirted canned cheese into his mouth. "Couldn't we go on a nice, bright Sunday morning? Maybe the Sunnyview Spirit likes to sleep in and we can catch him napping?"

"Ghosts don't sleep. And neither does the battle against bad guys and evil," Captain Awesome replied. "Halloween night is perfect. It's the one night a year we can go out after dark. . . ."

"I guess we can wear our superhero outfits as our 'costumes' so that Spirit guy never knows we're really superheroes," Nacho Cheese Man added.

"Exactly! And we'll go straight to the haunted house while the rest of the neighborhood will be

distracted by the awesome power of cavity-causing . . ."

"CANDY!" Both heroes jumped to their feet and shouted at the same time, bonking their heads on the bottom of the slide.

"I suppose we *could* go trick-or-treating to a few houses first," Captain Awesome said, rubbing his head.

"Yeah. I mean, it couldn't hurt." Nacho Cheese Man agreed faster

THWACK!

BONK!

than he had agreed with anything else in his life. "We could always use the extra . . . um . . ."

"Energy?" Captain Awesome offered.

"Yeah! That's it. Energy!"

"So we'll trick-or-treat at a few houses *first*," Captain Awesome repeated. "Get some candy to give us some . . . *energy*. . . ."

"But let's skip Mrs. Humbert's house," Nacho Cheese Man suggested. "She only gives out toothbrushes and pennies.

Can't fight a ghost with a toothbrush and a penny. Wait a second. What *do* you use to fight a ghost?"

"Well, I guess we'll just have to read every single issue of Super Dude again to see if he has any pointers," Captain Awesome replied, eager to find any excuse he could to reread his old issues.

And so the super plan was made. Costumes! Trick-or-treating! Skipping Mrs. Humbert and her toothbrushes and pennies! Haunted house! But as Captain Awesome and Nacho Cheese Man broke out some Super Dude comics that they both just happened to keep in their backpacks for emergencies, neither one noticed a pair of high-top sneakers peeking out from a nearby tree.

Someone sneaky had been listening!

CHAPTER 8

Getting Coco-Nutty

By
Eugene

HALLOWEEN!

It was every kid's dream come true and every parent's worst nightmare: free candy! And as much as you could stuff into your plastic pumpkin! There was only one goal: get enough candy to last until Easter. Oh, sure, you had Valentine's Day squeezed in there, but everyone knew Valentine's Day "candy" was just hard, sugary chalk. And Valentine's Day was the holiday of the most evil color in the world—pink!

"Safety flashlights?" Captain Awesome asked Nacho Cheese Man as the two heroes stood in front of Eugene's house going over their final checklist.

"Check."

"Safety glow sticks?"

"Check."

"Safety reflective tape?"

"Check."

"Safety parent?"

Nacho Cheese Man looked over at Captain Awesome's dad, Ned, who stood at the end of the driveway wearing a shiny gold jumpsuit,  fake sideburns, and sunglasses. He kept insisting that the boys call him "Elvis."

"But just remember, Elvis, you can *only* have the candies that have coconut in them!" Captain Awesome reminded his dad.

"Ew. Coconut," Nacho Cheese Man agreed. "They only put coconut in candy so adults have something to eat."

Nacho Cheese Man was right, for he knew that all coconut candy was the creation of Coco Nut, the evil candymaker who put gross things like coconut and cherries into otherwise perfectly good chocolate, hoping to create the ultimate evil: candy that tasted terrible!

The two heroes grabbed their pillowcases, hopped onto their bikes, and rode off down the street.

At every corner, "Elvis" waited for them, not only to make sure they were safe, but to search their bags for any candy that might contain the dreaded coconut and to eat it all, saving the two heroes from the Coco Nut's coco-nutty plan.

It was a tough job, but someone had to do it.

CHAPTER 9

The Headless Head of the Sunnyview Spirit!

By Eugene

Eugene's dad stood at the corner, where parents had gathered to watch their children trick-or-treat down the street and back.

The sun disappeared behind the trees, and the street slowly began to change. The brightness of day was replaced by creeping shadows. Flashlights clicked on. Glow sticks were snapped and shaken.

Captain Awesome and Nacho

ese Man rode the MI-TEE
bile and the Cheesy Rider to
the spooky house at the end of the
street. In the daytime it was creepy,
but now, with the yard wrapped in

darkness, the house looked like it was waiting to swallow any trick-or-treater foolish enough to step onto the porch.

GULP!

The two heroes leaned their bikes against the squeaky, broken fence, took a deep breath, and dug deep into their pillowcases full of chocolatey, energy-boosting candy. They each pulled out a Super Dude Super Crunch Bar full of nougatty goodness and little crunchy things. Nacho Cheese Man squirted some new pumpkin-flavored Halloween cheese onto his Super Crunch Bar, then offered the can to Captain Awesome.

"No, thanks," Captain Awesome whispered. "I don't mess with perfection."

"I'm ready when you are," said Nacho Cheese Man.

"Then let's get MI-TEE!" Captain Awesome whispered loudly. The superheroes made their way through the twisted trees and long grass toward the front door.

CREAK! CREAK! CREAK!

Each step up one of the porch stairs was met with the loud noise of old, splintered steps.

So much for sneaking up on the ghost, Captain Awesome thought.

They stopped at the top step. The only thing louder than Captain Awesome's heart pounding in his chest was Nacho Cheese Man's heart pounding in his. Captain Awesome took a step onto the porch.

MEOW!
SCREAM!
RUN!

The two heroes bolted down the steps and tumbled into a heap at the horrible sound of . . . a *cat?*

"Hey! That's Mr. Whiskersworth!" Captain Awesome whispered. "Sally's cat! What's he doing *here*?"

Mr. Whiskersworth scampered onto the porch and sat, licking his paws.

Captain Awesome jumped to his feet. "He's here to lead the charge! Come on! Let's go! CHAAARRRGE!" Nacho Cheese Man shouted, wildly squirting

the pumpkin-flavored Halloween cheese all over the place.

"MI-TEEEEEEEEEEE!" Captain Awesome yelled while trying to avoid being hit by wildly squirted pumpkin-flavored Halloween cheese. "By the authority of the Sunnyview Superhero Squad, we command you to show your headless head, Sunnyview Spirit!"

CREAK!

Captain Awesome's eyes went wide. It was just like in his dream.

GROAN!

And then, from around the corner of the house, came something that was not a cat! It raised its arms above its head. In the light of the full moon, Captain Awesome and Nacho Cheese Man could see that it was . . .

A GHOST!
THE SUNNYVIEW SPIRIT!

CHAPTER 10

The Rotten Plan of Princess Pinky from Ponytopia!

By
Eugene

"Oooooooh!" the Sunnyview
Spirit groaned.

Captain Awesome and Nacho
Cheese Man were stunned. They
stood on the porch like two cos-
tumed statues as the Sunnyview
Spirit crept closer.

STOMP!
STOMP!
STOMP!

Suddenly something jumped

between Captain Awesome, Nacho Cheese Man, and the Sunnyview Spirit! It was hard to tell in the moonlight, but it looked to be the same superhero who had saved Eugene's spelling bee trophy!

"Hold it right there!" the mystery hero said to the Sunnyview Spirit, her sneakers glowing bravely in the moonlight.

"Aaaah!" the ghost shouted, and fell backward.

Aaaah? Captain Awesome thought. *What kind of a ghost says "Aaaah!"?*

And then Captain Awesome saw something that made him gasp. The Sunnyview Spirit was wearing pink slippers!

"There's only one person *I* know who'd wear pink slippers on

Halloween . . . or ever!" Captain Awesome said as he reached down and yanked a white sheet off of the supposed Sunnyview Spirit.

"*Meredith Mooney?*" Nacho Cheese Man and the mystery hero said, gasping.

"Get your hands off me, you stinky stinkers!" Meredith shouted.

She jumped to her feet and adjusted her pink princess dress.

Then she pulled out a pink plastic tiara and angrily put it on her head. "You made me bend my tiara!"

"What are *you* doing here, Meredith?" Captain Awesome asked. "Or should I say . . . Little Miss Stinky Pinky?!"

"I'll have you know that *I* am Princess Pinky from the Planet

Ponytopia," Meredith announced, turning up her nose.

"More like Princess Pukey from the Planet *Gross*topia," Nacho Cheese Man replied.

"When I heard you in the cafeteria talking about coming to the house, I decided to scare you guys by dressing up as a ghost," Meredith proudly confessed.

"But what about the Sunnyview Spirit?" Captain Awesome asked.

"I made that up. My sister never got past the fence. She was too scared," Meredith explained. "But you guys can't tell my mom!" she whined. "Please, please, please!"

"I don't know . . . ," Captain Awesome said. "Trying to scare us was pretty rotten. I think your mom might want to know what you did."

"I'll give you all my candy!" Meredith pleaded.

"DEAL!" all three superheroes replied at once.

"You're free to go, Miss Stinky Pinky," Captain Awesome began, "but you must promise to be good and never—"

"Yeah, fine, be good, whatever, I promise,"Meredith said as she ran

from the house. She paused briefly at the broken fence to stick her tongue out one last time at Captain Awesome, Nacho Cheese Man, and the mystery hero.

CHAPTER II

The Mystery Hero Mystery . . . Solved!

By
Eugene

"**H**ow did you know we'd be here?" Captain Awesome asked the mystery hero.

"I heard you guys making your plans," she said. "Thought it might be a good idea to come in case you needed backup. But I better go—"

"Wait!" Captain Awesome said, stopping her. "This is the second time you've helped us, and we don't even know your name!"

"You can call me Supersonic Sal. This is my sidekick, Funny Cat."

Nacho Cheese Man elbowed Captain Awesome. "Ask her," Nacho Cheese Man whispered.

"No, *you* ask her," Captain Awesome whispered back.

"No, *you!*"

"Ask me what?" Supersonic Sal said.

"Well, since you've proven yourself to be a skilled superhero *twice*, we'd like to know if you want to join the Sunnyview Superhero Squad," said Captain Awesome.

"Yeah! We do all kinds of cool stuff like go on patrol, fight evil, and eat lots of brownies!" Nacho Cheese Man added.

"Sure," Supersonic Sal said coolly. "I'll catch you guys later!"

Sal headed for

the front gate, where her bike was. Funny Cat scampered after her.

"Hey! What's your real name?" Captain Awesome called out, but Supersonic Sal didn't reply. She just rode down the street in a flash.

"I guess we'll never know her real name . . . ," Nacho Cheese Man said, sighing.

"Or will we?" Captain Awesome said with a grin as Supersonic Sal rode her bike up the driveway to Sally Williams's house and raced inside. Both boys couldn't help but laugh. All this time the mystery hero had been Sally!

"I don't even think Super Dude could've figured that one out!" Nacho Cheese Man said.

The superheroes walked over to their bikes. They looked back

at the old house before they left. It was still the same house that had haunted Eugene's nightmare, but now that they had faced their fears, it just didn't seem so spooky anymore. Captain Awesome reached into his pillowcase and pulled out two Super Dude Super Crunch Bars. He handed one bar to Nacho Cheese Man.

Evil had been defeated, and there was still time to stock up on candy. Captain Awesome knew there was only word for a moment like this:

THE

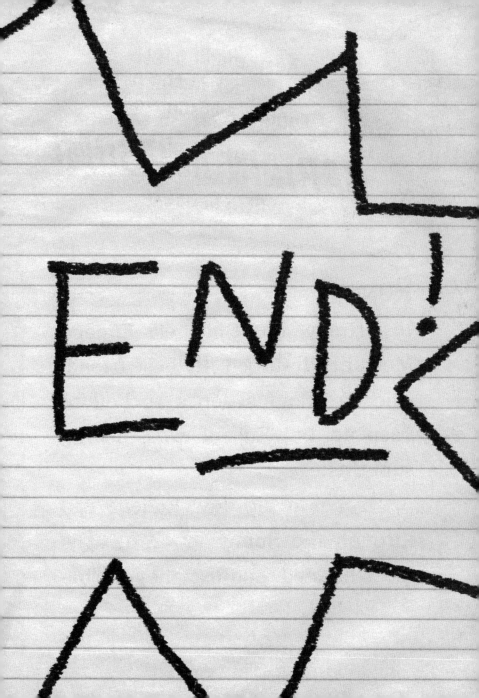

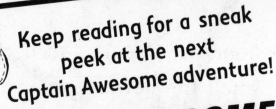

Keep reading for a sneak peek at the next Captain Awesome adventure!

CAPTAIN AWESOME
GETS CRUSHED

RUN!

"Hurry up, Charlie!" Eugene McGillicudy urged his best friend. Charlie Thomas Jones rushed to keep up, but Eugene was moving superfast.

It was a big day! Eugene ran through the Sunnyview Mall. His feet thudded against the marble floor. His heart raced. He could smell the new comic books like a dog smells bacon.

YUM!

This was all because today was **New Comic Book Day!**

I love the sound of that, Eugene thought. Then he thought it again.

New Comic Book Day!

It was the greatest day ever for Eugene, Charlie, and all comic book fans—the day when all the new comic books for the week came out. It was like Christmas, wrapped up in a birthday, in a bucket of Halloween candy.